HIDE AND SEEK

ON THE TRAIL WITH ORRIN PORTER ROCKWELL

Marc Otte

Deputy U.S. Marshals McGreggor and Garret Return for a Deadly Game of Cat and Mouse in Alaska's Rugged and Unforgiving Wilderness.

PO Box 221974 Anchorage, Alaska 99522-1974

ISBN 1-888125-53-5

Library of Congress Catalog Card Number: 99-69007

Copyright 1999 by Marc Otte
—First Edition—

All rights reserved, including the right of reproduction in any form, or by any mechanical or electronic means including photocopying or recording, or by any information storage or retrieval system, in whole or in part in any form, and in any case not without the written permission of the author and publisher.

Cover painting by Richard A. Cook
Other art by Marc Otte

Manufactured in the United States of America.

FOR LOU

ACKNOWLEDGMENTS

It would have been difficult, if not impossible, for me to have written this book by myself. So, in that vein I give a few folks their due thanks: First, my wife Victoria for her constant encouragement and patience; my daughter Catelyn, for listening to the entire manuscript read out loud; Ty Cunningham for sharing his tracking and martial arts knowhow; Deborah Luper for her help with the Athabascan language; my pilot friends, Bill Fisher, Kevin Guinn, Richard Cobb, and Ken Allen for sharing their expertise in the fine art of Alaska bush flying; all the deputies and staff of the United States Marshals Service District of Alaska, for allowing me to constantly bounce my ideas off them (even when they had no idea that's what I was doing); my editor Marthy Johnson, who gives inspiration as well as much needed criticism; and finally, my publisher, Evan Swensen, who believed in me enough to help me learn.

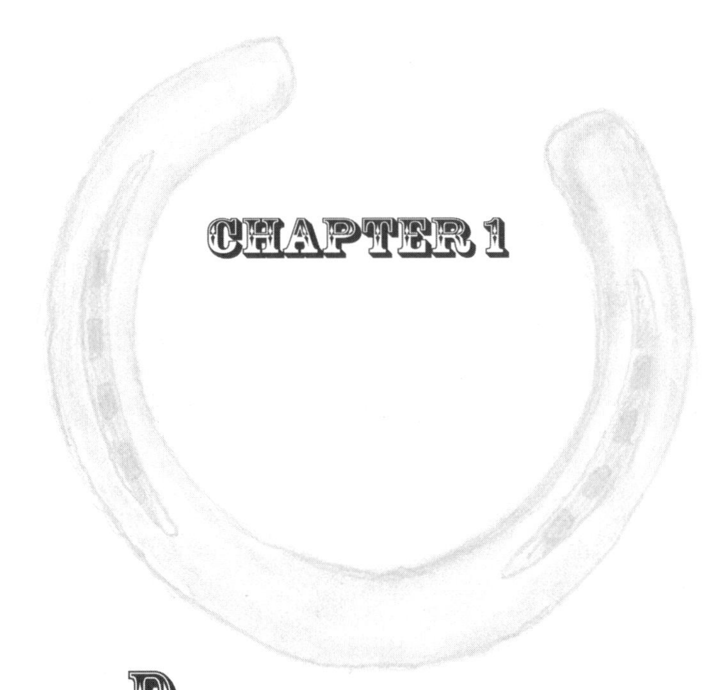

CHAPTER 1

Deputy U.S. Marshal, Skip Garret, knew it was going to be a bad day when his barber got the hiccups and lopped a hunk of hair the size of a golf ball off the top of his head. That didn't matter so much because he would just cover it with hat anyway, but the heel came off his boot on his way out of the shop, and he had to gimp the rest of the way to his pickup. Garret truly considered it bad luck when the heel just fell off a boot. He had to stand at the repair shop counter for twenty minutes in his sock while the heel was repaired. Then Brick decided to take his sweet time loading in the horse trailer (something Skip refused to rush), which put him an hour and a half behind schedule getting to the mountains above Lolo—and now he'd lost the trail.

It was impossible. Tracks didn't just end—unless there was a horse standing in them. Garret adjusted the .45 caliber revolver on his belt so it wouldn't bang against the back of his high-cantled saddle, and gave his sorrel a pat on the neck. The horse, the color of a new copper penny—with not so much as a speck of white—let out a long, rattling snort and pawed the ground with an impatient forefoot.

Skip's daddy always told him a man should stick to things he was good at. The elder Garret had never been averse to the idea of his only son learning new things. The man merely believed that if you found yourself blessed with a true talent, you ought to use it. For Skip, horsemanship fell right at the top of that category. Hunting outlaws ran a close second. Unfortunately, tracking didn't seem to fit into his talent inventory at all. He'd already been on this particular set of tracks for the last hour and up to now believed he was closing in on his quarry. A half hour before, the gelding had perked up and Skip thought he was close, but working on through the thick fir forest all he'd found was more horse tracks scuffing the dusty, needle-littered ground.

About a hundred feet back the tracks made an unmistakable circle in a clearing the size of a small kitchen. They started off again in the same direction, though, so Skip kept following them, scanning the area for booby traps or signs of ambush. He wished he had Belle, his blue heeler dog, with him. She was an excellent tracker and together they could have had this whole business over with by now. Kate had taken her to the vet for a checkup and shots, so she was out of the picture for the day at least.

Compared to humans, horses were relatively easy to follow; particularly shod horses like the one he was tracking now. The heavy, metal shoes dug deep gouges in the forest floor and even a novice like Skip could follow them with little trouble—until now. At the edge of a broad clearing, the tracks stopped. They didn't veer off or jump further out into the dry grass, they just stopped as if horse and rider had vanished into the warm mountain air.

Skip urged his horse a few steps out into the clearing, then back again, looking at the deep tracks he made in the soft grass. He felt the hair on the back of his neck prickle and glanced around at the shadowy line of evergreens. The tangle of jack pine, hemlock, and buckbrush made it impossible to see more than twenty or thirty feet. It would be an easy place to hide but a difficult place to take a horse. The deputy took a comb out of his shirt pocket and ran it slowly through his chocolate brown handlebar mustache. Kate called it his thinking habit and still giggled at the way he did it when he ruminated deeply over some task.

"Well, Brick," Skip whispered to his gelding, "the way I figure it, he either got off his horse and ate it right here or he's doubled back on us. Yep, that's exactly what he's done, doubled back I think." Skip groaned quietly to himself. His ribs still ached from the injuries he got bringing in a bunch of killers from the Cabinet mountains the previous fall. Riding itself was getting to be almost painless, but getting on and off reminded him he had wounds that were almost a year old. At thirty-four, Skip was far from an old man, but it sure took him longer to heal now than it did when he was riding broncs back in high school.

Taking care not to step on any sign, the tall lawman stayed in close to his horse in case he needed to remount in a hurry. He leaned backward a bit to stretch the muscles around his rib cage and gave the surrounding trees another just-in-case look before bending down to study the tracks. This tracking alone stuff could be downright dangerous. If you concentrated too much on the ground someone was likely to sneak up and make things just a bit unpleasant.

The forest floor was a mosaic of pooled light and shadow under a thick canopy of fir and hemlock. No birds sang. The squirrels normally chattering in the trees were silent. Except for the rhythmic sound of Brick's heavy breathing and the creaking groan of saddle leather, the place was quiet as an empty church.

In truth, Skip hated this sneaking around stuff, preferring an all-out frontal charge to anything else. Still, there were times—though he couldn't think of many— when this sort of thing was needed. Hanging on to his horse, the deputy squatted next to the line of tracks and used the tail end of his braided cotton reins to trace the outline of the last impression.

A voice came from trees to his right, a soft but piercing rasp. "What does the sign say to you?"

Skip stared down at the ground and shrugged. "It tells me, my friend Terry, that you taught the dun mare to fly right about—here." Skip tapped the track with the tip of a rein. "I figured you were hiding somewhere out there watching me."

"Only for a minute or two," said Deputy Terry McGreggor, Skip's partner and friend for the past five years. His black hat was tossed back over his shoulders against the horsehair stampede string and his bald head glistened with sweat in the diffused light of the afternoon. "Don't be too hard on yourself. I had a pretty good head start on you this time."

Skip stood from the track and stretched his back. "Where's the dun mare?" Even though Terry had more or less adopted the powerful little mare, she was still Skip's horse and he liked to keep track of her.

"I left her nibbling twigs about two hundred yards that way." Terry nodded over his shoulder. "Didn't want you to cheat and let Brick do all the work."

Tipping his hat back, Skip grinned. "Are you going to tell me how you did this or keep it a secret all day?"

Terry motioned over his shoulder with a leather gloved hand. "Remember that circle of tracks back a ways?"

Skip nodded.

Terry drew a rough map in the dirt with the toe of his boot. "All I did was ride to the edge of this clearing then put the mare in reverse back to the circle. Once we got there I hopped her over that long dead fall on the right side of the trail where you wouldn't see her tracks unless you got off your horse and looked."

Skip rolled his eyes and shook his head. "Foiled by staying in the saddle. Horse back hide and seek wasn't as tiring when I was a kid." His dislike for doing anything from the ground that he could do from the back of a horse was almost legendary. Many was the time he'd startled the counter help at the Burger Heaven on the outskirts of Missoula by riding a horse to the drive-up window to place his order.

In a few minutes Terry retrieved the dun mare and both men re-walked the trail. McGreggor was an expert tracker and pointed out a whole list of signs gone completely unnoticed; how the track looked when the horse was moving forward versus backing up, the way the underbrush was separated where he jumped the log and disappeared into the forest. Tracking was right at the top of Terry's talent list.

The tracking lesson over for the day, the men remounted. Skip, tired from spending so much time afoot, and eager to work Brick a little harder before he went home, reined up next to his friend on the mare. "I say enough of this fiddle footin' around. How about a little race over to Cow Creek?" He didn't really care where they raced to, but Cow Creek was in the opposite direction of the trailer and Skip was particular about not running his horses home

"You think you have time?" Terry stopped the dun mare in her tracks.

Skip shrugged. "Sure. Kate will be at the vet's for another half hour. Besides, Brick and I feel all cooped up inside after all that slow, steady tracking stuff."

Terry looked at his watch, then opened his mouth as if to say something but the words turned into a war whoop. He turned the mare on her haunches and tore back up the trail toward the clearing, his black hat flying in the wind behind him held by the stampede strings.

Skip clucked in Brick's ear but there was no need. As soon as the horse realized Skip wanted to go, he was airborne. It wasn't so much that the gelding didn't want to be left alone. Skip's company was plenty good for him. But he had a winning heart and if given the opportunity wasn't about to let any other horse, including the dun mare, get anywhere before he did. Without that quality, Skip never would have bought him in the first place.

By the time they got to the far edge of the clearing, the stout horse had nearly caught the fleet little mare. By leaning well out over her neck, Terry was able to keep the edge and spur ahead on the dark forest trail. Skip was less than thirty feet away when he saw dust fly and the mare's broad rump duck into a screeching halt. It was all he could do to keep Brick from plowing into her.

Throwing his feet out in front of him to keep from flying out of the saddle, Skip leaned back against the reins and they skittered to a stop with Brick's nose only inches from the mare's tail. He opened his mouth to complain about Terry clogging the road--until he saw why the mare stopped so suddenly.

Ahead of them, atop a handsome roman-nosed bay, sat their old friend and guardian angel of sorts, Orrin Porter Rockwell. The old man stood in his stirrups and craned his neck, looking up the trail behind the two deputies. His long white hair and flowing beard moved little in the afternoon breeze. Dressed in a tan woolen vest and homespun cotton shirt, Rockwell, looked, and was a man out of time. A smartly creased grey felt hat tipped back to reveal a gleaming forehead.

"You boys all right?" He continued to check their back trail. "If someone's a-chasin' you, feel free to take your leave. Don't wait around and get yourselves killed on my account."

Terry raised a gloved hand and smiled. "No one's after us, Port. We're just having a little race." He glanced over at Skip, who was grinning like a cat at the prospect of reuniting with their heavenly friend.

Rockwell relaxed and sat back in the saddle. "Glad to hear it. I got wind you boys were fixin' to get in some sort of a jackpot, so I hopped aboard old Jake here and came a-runnin'. When I saw you tearing across the flat like that I thought sure I'd see a mob break outta the trees right behind you."

"No," Skip said, a little embarrassed that he wasn't doing something more important than racing a horse when his hero came to call on him. He wanted to change the subject. "Just a friendly contest. It's good to see you though. I was beginning to think you'd forgotten about us."

It had been months since the two deputies had received a visit from their old friend and it startled them to be suddenly face to face with the great Mormon gunfighter.

"Good to see you, too." Rockwell leaned forward in the saddle and crossed his arms on the horn. "Time goes by pretty fast for me up there, I reckon, so I shouldn't complain, but I get bored easy." The old man removed his hat and took on a more conspiratorial tone. "I probably shouldn't be blabbin' about this but the spirit world is a little shy in the adventure department."

The excitement of the race and shock of seeing Rockwell had caused Skip to outrun his wits a little and it wasn't until they caught back up that the old gunfighter's words began to dawn on him. "Hang on a minute. You said you heard we were in some sort of trouble."

"I did indeed." Rockwell smoothed back his long silver-grey hair and replaced his hat.

Skip raised an eyebrow. "Well, I've gotta say I don't like the sound of that. The last time you forecast trouble I got thrown off a mountain."

Port shrugged and gave a squinty grin. "And you loved every minute of it. I don't really know what to tell you. I heard you were in trouble so I came a-runnin' What are you boys up to lately that might spell doom and such?"

Terry leaned over in the saddle to stretch. He was beginning to get stiff and considered stiffness the mortal enemy of a martial artist. He shook his head. "I can't think of anything any more dangerous than usual."

Rockwell looked over at Skip who was combing his mustache.

The deputy shrugged. "I'm working on a few drug fugitives ...

some pretty bad actors I guess. I suppose it could have something to do with them."

"No tellin'," Rockwell said. "I didn't stick around for any of the details." He stretched tall and took a deep breath. Smiling at his two friends he suddenly focused sharply on Skip. "Say, how'd it all work out with that Beebe gal?"

Skip grinned. "Her name's Garret now."

Terry gave Rockwell a wink. "Been married nine months and already expecting a little Garret."

"I'm happy for you Brother Skip. A man like you needs a good woman to quiet his soul."

"Amen to that," Terry said, nodding to his friend.

Jake's head came up and Rockwell prepared to turn. "Well, gotta git. I'm glad to be back in the hunt whatever this is all about. The fact is, it's not the bear on the trail that usually kills you. It's the doggone snake in the grass. So you boys just watch your P's and Q's and I'll do my level best to watch your hind sides."

Skip smiled at his partner. They accepted, had even grown used to a certain amount of risk and danger in their chosen way of life. Both men were vigilant and took care of each other. If their hind sides needed watching though, neither man could think of anyone better to do the job than Orrin Porter Rockwell.

CHAPTER 2

Deputy Marshal Garret tipped back the broad brim of his silver belly hat and twirled the curly end of his mustache while he surveyed the dim, smoke-filled bar. Plenty of ne'er-do-wells and malingerers decorated the noisy room, most of which, for one reason or another, looked like they needed arresting. The Double Bubble wasn't one of those classy joints springing up around Missoula, where upscale yuppie and cowboy types could stop after work to share a drink and nibble a few salty snacks. The Bubble was a bar where, if you didn't have a big knife when you came in, they issued you one at the front door. Some people went there to sell stolen loot, some to hide from the law, but most just wanted to get drunk.

Across the barroom a wannabe outlaw biker type with a ragged denim vest and thinning black hair played pool with a greasy, blonde woman of undeterminable age. In the low shadows it was hard for Skip to be sure, but it looked like the guy had more tattoos than he had teeth. Though he was more than likely wanted for something, the biker wasn't the deputy's target.

Mordekai Yeager was best known for the peculiar habit of parking his bottom row of teeth in front of his uppers. The resulting jut of his lower jaw along with his height of over six-feet-eight and his characteristic smell, something close to rotten bananas, made Mordekai easy to pick out in a crowd. The trouble was, he didn't happen to be in this particular crowd.

A small mob of four or five potbellied men hovered under a fuzzy television in the back corner, watching professional wrestling and alternately pounding their chests and guzzling beer. Others sat in motley groups of two or three nodding their heads to the beat of the steel guitar whining from the distorted stereo.

It was difficult to think, let alone concentrate on arresting someone as dangerous as Mordekai Yeager. His file said he had beaten a Bozeman policeman to within an inch of his life while Mordekai was still a teenager.

Yeager's last run-in with the law had been an assault against a bartender on Tlingit Indian land outside Sitka, Alaska. For that, the giant had served a stint in the federal prison in Sheridan, Oregon, then neglected to contact his parole officer back in Anchorage upon his release. The parole officer took a dim view of that and promptly petitioned the judge for a warrant, which was sent to the U.S. Marshals for service in Montana where Yeager was believed to have family.

"You want a beer or something?" A tired waitress with drawn-on eyes glared through the haze at Skip and his partner. She was short and bony and had a weary look even her abundant face paint couldn't hide.

"No thanks," Skip smiled up at her. "We're just waiting for a friend."

The woman rolled her dark eyes and wheeled back toward the crowded bar with an impatient snort.

"My mama would bawl her head off if she knew the kind of places I hang out in these days," Skip said under his breath to no one in particular. Twirling the ice in his three-dollar ginger ale with a little plastic stick, he looked across the small table. If the close atmosphere of the bar was bothering Skip, he was certain it wasn't doing Terry McGreggor any good either.

Terry sat across the tippy table staring at the front door, his bald head reflecting the blue and orange light of a neon beer sign buzzing on the clapboard wall behind him. Fiery green eyes probed the darkness through narrow slits, missing no one who came into the smoky room. "There's not enough air in here for all of us," he muttered without shifting his gaze on the entrance.

Terry was a man of discipline, and watching so many people who lacked the trait put him in a sullen mood.

Any normal man who came through the swinging door and spied Deputy Terry McGreggor with his dark, drooping mustache, wearing his hunting face, would've promptly turned on his heels and figured on a better place to be—but the Double Bubble wasn't exactly overflowing with normal folks.

"What do you figure?" Skip asked, leaning across the teetering table. "Should we wait another hour?"

Terry shrugged, his eyes still burning a hole in the front door. "So far I've watched three drug deals go down and two guns that are probably stolen get sold to the bartender. I don't relish the idea of leaving without who we came in for."

Skip nodded. "I suppose. Do you think our guy Icky is trustworthy?"

"Guess so, he's your informant. You swore by him thirty minutes ago. He said he didn't know when but he seemed certain enough Yeager would be by sometime tonight. Besides, if he doesn't show, Icky doesn't get his money." Terry looked at his watch. "It's ten thirty. I'm sure our cover will wear off completely by eleven. Then we can get you back home to your blushing bride before you turn into a pumpkin."

"I don't care if we stay till midnight," Skip lied. Reality was a lot different than action shows he watched on television. Spending time on a stakeout to catch a bad hombre was all well and good, but he had a life. "If he's not here by then, I'm all for making tracks." He took a swig of his soda and dabbed at his bushy mustache with a red bandanna. The Bubble wasn't a place you could trust to provide clean napkins.

Skip and Kate had been married more than nine months and she was well past the blushing stage. She did miss him on the late-night stakeouts, though, and he saw no reason to waste time sitting around in a stinking bar where half the people already knew he was lawman anyway. "I guess most people have figured out we're not plain old beer-swilling customers by now. I say midnight's our drop-dead time."

Terry tapped the table between them with his forefinger and winked a narrow eye toward the door. I don't think we'll have to wait that long. Our mope just came in with two friends in tow."

Skip didn't turn around, but watched the movement in Terry's eyes. Yeager and his two companions made their way to the bar and then to the dart board. By turning his chair just a bit, Skip was able to get a good look at the scene.

A dart game was already in progress between a lanky blond kid—who would have needed a fake I.D. to get into a more reputable place—and a slender redhead wearing enough green eye shadow Skip could see it clearly from their table. She looked at least three times the kid's age. With the loud music and murmur in the bar it was impossible to tell what Mordekai was saying to the boy, but it was clear he wanted quick use of the dart board. The outlaw, almost seven feet tall, hovered above the skinny kid who clutched his darts so hard two of their feathers fell off and fluttered to the grimy concrete floor.

Mordekai's friends leaned back against the end of the bar and laughed at the frightened boy. One of the men was almost as tall as Yeager himself and looked to be in better shape. He wore no jacket and his powerful arms and broad shoulders flexed under a dark T-shirt. His jet-black hair was greased back in a short ponytail and he sported a heavy gold chain around a thick bullish neck. Apart from a slight grin at the corners of his hairless upper lip the man's face was passive, almost pleasant. Looking nice but thinking mean, Skip called it. Not recognizing it was the downfall of many an otherwise good policeman. Terry noted the big man's lack of a jacket and nodded to himself. He'd much rather deal with someone who liked to show off his muscles than someone who might be hiding a gun.

"That pug there to the left must be a boxer," Skip said, nodding toward the shorter of Yeager's companions. "I'll bet that guy's got one serious snoring problem."

The pug's bulbous nose was smeared all over the front of his face. It had obviously been broken more than once. Though dwarfed by Yeager and the other man, the pug was no runt. Had it not been for the ponderous belly completely hiding his western belt buckle, he would have been formidable. Even as overweight as he was, he seemed the more dangerous of the two at the bar. The man had obviously been tested in actual battle with someone at least capable of breaking his nose. Terry doubted that Mr. Ponytail, on the other hand, was much more than a bully who muscled his way through life without having to fight because of his size. He'd seen the type over and over again in his martial arts classes and they proved the old harder-they-fall adage.

"I'd like to take him when he goes outside or to the bathroom," Skip said, downing the last of his ginger ale and crunching a piece of ice. "This bar room crowd is chancy and somebody's liable to get hurt."

"I agree," Terry nodded. "But it looks like we may not get that luxury."

The blond youngster with the darts would likely have loved to relinquish the board to someone as mean and ugly as Mordekai Yeager but the redheaded barfly kept egging him on. She had no loyalty to the boy and would just as easily have gone with Yeager. The bony kid was too inexperienced to see he was nothing more than a little evening entertainment for the bar. Booze and the attentions of his newfound girlfriend had filled him with counterfeit manhood and he couldn't bear to back down. He turned his shaking head toward the bar as if he expected to find some help. Mordekai stuck his square chin out even further and glowered down at the boy shouting some slurred epithet that was lost in the hum of voices and clattering glass. The big outlaw's facial features were almost lost between his prominent jaw and brow.

"I'll bet he was an ugly baby." Skip scooted back his chair and got to his feet. It was painfully clear there would be a fight and that shut down any opportunity to take the outlaw away from his friends. It wasn't that either deputy was scared. There was just an easy way and a hard way to do things. In front of his friends, Yeager might make the same mistake the kid was making and pick the hard way.

"You break the news to our outlaw," Terry said, putting on his black, flat-brimmed hat. He pulled a chain up from his collar and let the badge on the end of it hang down in the center of his chest. "I'll watch his two buddies."

Terry strode easily toward the bar, his arms relaxed and swinging naturally. The crowd parted before him as if he had the plague when they noticed the shiny circle-star hanging on his chest. Showing the badge to the mousy brunette behind the bar, he told her to kill the music and stand next to the back wall—which she promptly did.

The effect of no music after such a clamor was better than beating a gong for getting everyone's attention. Even Mordekai, who had lifted the skinny kid off the ground by his shirt collar, turned to stare at the bartender to see what had gone wrong with the stereo.

Skip felt for his revolver, just to make sure it was where he had left it under his jacket and pulled the badge out of his own shirt. When he was still twenty feet away he held it up in his left hand.

"Mordekai Yeager!" Skip said in a firm, drawling voice. The outlaw's head snapped around. He was more than a little drunk and a trickle of crystalline drool dripped from the corner of his sagging mouth.

"U.S. marshals. Put the boy down and keep your hands where I can see them. You're under arrest."

No one moved. Yeager slowly blinked at Skip, turning his head from side to side as if trying to bring Skip into focus.

"I have a warrant for you out of the District of Alaska." It was quiet enough in the bar now so Skip didn't have to yell. He and Terry had planned for this sort of response. From what they had been told, Yeager would need things lined out for him a number of times.

The huge outlaw still held on to the young dart player as he glared hard at Skip. The slow-moving gears in his brain were almost audible while he thought of a way out of his new predicament. He raised a bushy eyebrow. "Why, I've spent my whole life here in Montana," he slurred in a deep, croaking voice. "What if I tell you I ain't never been to Alaska?"

"Might as well sit back and enjoy the trip then," Terry said from the bar. Yeager's pending fight with the boy had kept them from getting the backup he would have liked for a capture in such a rowdy spot. "It really is a beautiful state."

Yeager still held the kid up in front of him, a skinny shield. "Well then," he started with a jagged grin. "What if I say I ain't goin'?"

Skip snorted and shot a quick glance at Terry. "Oh Mordekai, Mordekai," The marshal said, shaking his head. "You're going alright. How you go is up to you." Skip pointed an open hand at the bar. "And how many of your friends go with you is up to them. But understand this, you're going."

A low growl welled up inside the giant and the sound of it, spilling out with his rotten breath scared the blonde kid so badly he jabbed the sharp end of the two darts he held into the front of Yeager's thigh. The big man stared blankly for the moment it took the pain message to make the long journey from leg to brain.

When it did, he bellowed like a crazed bull and dropped the boy, who had enough sense to crawl to safety behind the redhead. Keenly interested in the impending fight, the woman shooed him away without a second look.

Yeager might have been a slow thinker, but as it turned out, he was one heck of a dart player. Wrenching the darts from his thigh with a deep, guttural war cry, he threw them hard and fast; one at Skip and the other at Terry. Instinctively, Skip brought a hand up to his face and the dart struck him deep in the open palm. Terry merely turned his head slightly to the side and let the missile slip harmlessly past him. Skip saw his friend evade the dart out of the corner of his eye and chided himself. Terry was always harping on the benefits of merely getting out of the way rather than blocking things. Though Skip dearly loved a good scrap, he always felt a little self-conscious when Terry watched him. His teacher seeing him make a mistake hurt more than any dart.

Across the room, Terry though it best to deal with the problem of Mr. Pug first, whose beet-red nostrils already twitched and flared as he drew himself into a compact boxer's crouch. Terry had little doubt that the boxer would be the first of the two to attack. The man had been in fights before and treated it as his sworn duty to get this one underway.

Through years of practice, the stout little deputy had learned that fighting two people wasn't as hard as it would seem. In fact, many times he preferred it. People who attacked two against one rarely showed any discipline at all and got in each other's way more than they helped with the fight. In his experience, when the first opponent went down the second was so demoralized that he was fairly easy to contend with.

Mr. Ponytail stepped quickly to the side, grinning a slack-jawed grin, when Pug drew back for what he thought would be a quick knockout punch against the shorter deputy. Terry pulled his own weight up and prepared to move. When the blow was delivered, the deputy simply stepped around, letting it swoosh by only an inch from his face. Now, close at the boxer's side, Terry grabbed a handful of shirt collar and pushed the man the way his momentum already carried him. Spinning lightly on his feet Terry let the knife edge of his forward hand glide under the bulbous red nose, slamming hard into the upper lip and bringing the fat man to his tiptoes while arresting the forward motion. The lawman turned his body in a tight, fluid arc, first throwing his hand toward the ceiling, then toward the floor, carrying the pug's nose and him along with it—up and down—the Heaven-and-Earth throw.

The boxer landed on his back with a bone-jarring thud. The wind left his lungs and he struggled to draw a breath. He'd had the wind knocked out of him enough times he knew what to do to stay in the fight, but Terry kept him on the ground with a well placed boot toe to the nerve running up the side of his thigh. Pug writhed in pain among the peanut shells on the floor, dazed by the speed and ease with which the little deputy had put him down.

Given the snakes eye view of the bald marshal's boot toe, Pug moaned and raised his hands in surrender just as the muscle man in the black T-shirt lumbered in for a tackle. Terry floated quickly to the side so he could keep both opponents in view, forcing Mr. Ponytail to step over his partner. The obstacle didn't slow him down much but he stepped on an outstretched hand of the downed boxer, who yelped in pain.

"Last chance to give up," Terry said cheerfully, mostly to enrage the man and speed up the attack. The time for peaceful outcomes had long ago come and gone.

"You ..." The muscle man slurred as he closed the gap.

Aiming for the line of gold chain running alongside Ponytail's head, Terry whirled out of the way like a matador escaping a charging bull, and let the flat of his forearm slam into the side of his opponent's neck, just above his collar bone.

The effect was immediate and the muscles on the big man's entire right side quit taking orders from his brain. He collapsed on the ground in a spiraling twist, looking cross-eyed and confused. He tried to rise, but his legs wouldn't obey and he collapsed on the filthy floor.

The whole affair had taken less than ten seconds but was all the time Terry had. Skip might need help with Yeager, so this nonsense had to be ended quickly. The deputy took a quick step back and tapped the holster under his light jacket. It was one thing to scrap against two opponents in the dojo, but when you were making an arrest in a crowded bar, it was sometimes more prudent to slap leather.

"Hey, I'm just laying here minding my own business," the boxer moaned in a voice a little higher than Terry imagined it would've been. "I had no idea Mordy was a wanted man." Ponytail tried to speak but could only manage a croak. In the end, he raised his left hand in surrender, while the right hung useless and limp by his side.

Back with Yeager, Skip had his hands full. The fugitive had picked the hard way. Half waiting to see how his comrades were doing, Yeager, growled ferociously when he saw they would be no help. Crouching low, the giant rushed straight for Skip, who grabbed a teetering wooden table and shoved, pushing it forward like a shopping cart. The two men closed on each other fast and their combined weight of more than five hundred pounds hit Yeager right above the knees.

The flimsy wooden table all but evaporated between the two raging men and they slammed into each other like two angry bulls. Running into Mordekai Yeager was a lot like running into a Buick but Skip was no small fry himself. What the deputy lacked in the finesse of his partner, he made up for in pure, mad-dog meanness when he fought. Most people who knew Skip thought he had no temper at all. As he liked to put it, his fuse was hard to light, but once you did, stand back. It didn't take long to burn down.

When the two men collided, Yeager wrapped his arms around Skip in a bear hug, intent on squeezing the very life out of him. Before he could be lifted off the ground, the lawman stomped down hard, driving the hard heels of his boots into the other man's feet. Yeager roared and loosened his grip enough for Skip to give him a head butt and wriggle free. The fight had taken the two men across the crowded barroom to the pool table and Yeager snatched up a cue, brandishing it in front of him like a skinny baseball bat.

"Now you're done for, squirt," the outlaw bellowed, chopping straight down with the cue. Skip jumped to one side and narrowly missed getting brained. Instead, the light pine stick broke across his shoulder. Skip hardly felt the impact through his rage, but now Yeager had a more dangerous weapon in the sharp broken piece he still hung on to.

Grabbing a chair with both hands Skip pushed it forward like a lion tamer, fending off Yeager's pokes with the makeshift spear. The mountainous bad guy was too slow to feel much pain, but when Skip trapped his wrist between the chair legs and twisted, his eyes got wide and he dropped the weapon.

But Yeager was far from giving up. Before the broken cue even hit the ground, the outlaw wrapped his thick fingers around the base of the chair and gave it a rough yank. Skip let go and rolled toward the outlaw, going past him low and out of his reach.

"That is enough!," Skip said, drawing his stainless steel revolver with a hiss that could be heard even above Yeager's labored breathing. "On the ground!"

Yeager heard but was too slow to see how dangerous the deputy was and raised the chair high above his head as he turned. Before he could complete his turn, the heavy barrel of Skip's Smith and Wesson connected with a loud crack to the chunk of bone and gristle Yeager called a skull.

The outlaw blinked twice, the chair suspended above his head, his rummy brain trying to work out what had just happened. Then his legs buckled and he collapsed into a smelly heap on the barroom floor. The chair followed him down and gave him another rap on the noggin for good measure.

Skip prodded him with a boot toe and looked over at Terry before reholstering his weapon. Normal handcuffs wouldn't fit around Yeager's tree-trunk wrists but that was the great advantage of hunting known fugitives—you could plan ahead. Skip reached into the inside pocket of his jacket and pulled out a pair of leg irons with a chain he'd shortened on his anvil that morning. They worked perfectly.

"Not the most fluid I've ever seen you scrap," Terry said, removing his hat and wiping sweat from his bald head. "But I'll have to admit it was effective. I especially liked the laying on of hands with the Smith and Wesson"

Skip stood bent over, his hands on his knees, panting by his prisoner. "I think it was Wyatt Earp who said, better clunked on the head than dead. You know me Terry, I'm an easygoing guy if folks will just behave."

Terry chuckled. "You bet. Completely nonviolent. A real pussycat."

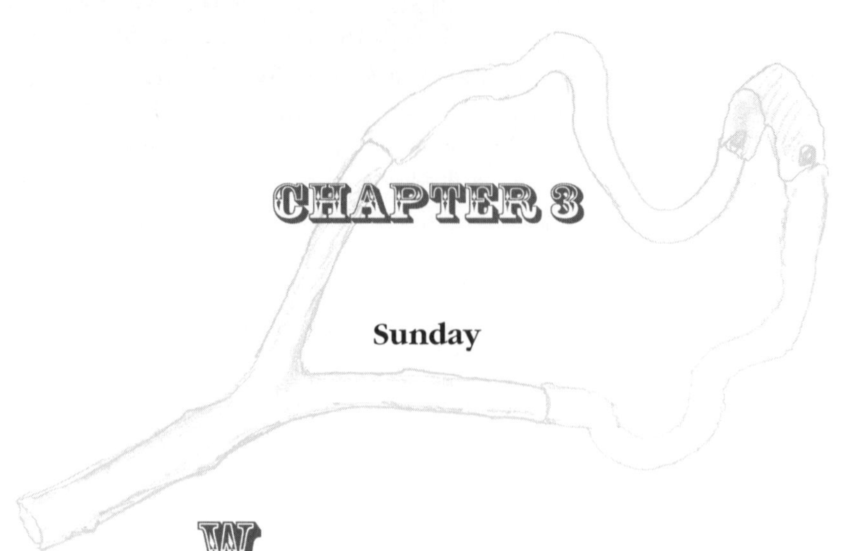

CHAPTER 3

Sunday

With their father gone, the burden of raising the two Fuller boys fell squarely on Tracy's shoulders. They were good boys and though she still cried herself to sleep two nights out of every three, she measured up to the task remarkably well. She had no trouble at all taking care of the day-to-day necessities of life. Financially they were fine. In that respect the state came through with flying colors after Wally's death, even providing enough to guarantee both boys a college education.

It was the smaller, more subtle things that troubled her. The "dad" things that she had a hard time understanding. Of course little Matt was still pretty easy to handle. He wasn't really old enough to get into much trouble and seemed perfectly happy to play alone or with friends when he wasn't playing with his mother. Paul, on the other hand, was beginning to show signs of all-out rebellion. He never mistreated Tracy herself; for the most part he treated her like a queen. However, the news from school wasn't good. More and more, reports of bad behavior kept coming in. Even his Primary teacher, Sister Martin, had mentioned his bad attitude. He always apologized, but nothing changed.

Terry and Skip came by often and helped when they could. They had taken Paul on a few campouts with the Scouts even though he was still only eleven and had a few months to go before he was supposed to go on overnighters. The Primary President threw a gigantic fit over it, as if a campout or two might ruin the boy's chances for eternal salvation. Tracy always smiled and remained polite, but it galled her that the rules came before the kids. After all, the woman had a husband and her boys still had a father.

About six months after Wally's murder, Tracy felt she needed a change. She thought about moving out of their little yellow house. In the end, though, she decided that the memories she'd first wanted to run from might be a better reason to stay. With all they had been through it seemed too cruel to drag the boys away from their friends and force them to make new ones.

So, she got a job. Kate Garret had recommended her as a substitute teacher at the junior high where she taught. It seemed to be just the thing to soothe her soul—during the day at least—and Tracy found she enjoyed getting her mind into something. She had even substituted eighth grade for two weeks back in December while Kate and Skip went to Cardston to get married and have a little honeymoon.

In a way, it was her substituting that caused the fight.

Paul Fuller had inherited his father's height so at eleven, he was a head taller than even the oldest boys in Primary. His voice was beginning to change and the high key of the Primary songs made him self-conscious. Each Sunday he grabbed his little brother by the hand and tried his best to make a hasty escape as soon as the last amen was said.

Today was Ward Conference so the halls were especially crowded and it was difficult to drag Matt along as quickly as he would have liked. Paul hated the halls almost as much as he hated Primary. He still got far too many sorrowful pats on the head for his taste. He wished people would just leave him alone.

Four teenage boys stood in the hall by the kitchen serving window. All but one sported the bowl style haircut that was so popular with the young men. Before his father died Paul had thought he might like to get his hair cut like that and maybe be a little more like the other boys. His dad had sat down by him in Sacrament Meeting one Sunday and gestured to the pew of Deacons and Teachers on the front row.

"You ought to offer those poor boys some money so they can buy themselves the rest of those haircuts they were trying to get," his dad said, patting him on the knee.

Paul had just smiled and scooted over next to the huge bear of a man and felt grateful for the plain old highway-patrol haircut his father respected.

Now he squeezed Matt's hand harder, urging him to hurry through the stuffy halls and past the boys.

"How about Sister Fuller? Did you have her for anything last year?" Asked a boy named Nick, a slouchy fourteen-year-old with a half-shaved bowl cut of carrot-colored hair.

Paul stopped when he heard the mention of his mother's name.

"Pre-algebra," one of the deacons said, shaking his head. He had seen the Fuller boys approach but Nick had not.

"What an old bag. I'm glad summer got here before I ever had her again. I'm just afraid she might go back to school and be a full time teacher before I graduate. I never had anyone as bad as her."

Matt looked up at his older brother, blinking. "Is he calling our Mama a bag?"

Paul had already let go of his little brother's hand and waded through the crowd of passers by to the group of boys. All of them stood wide eyed when they saw him approach. Most of the boys liked Paul and looked uncomfortable with the talk about Sister Fuller.

When Nick turned and saw Paul he merely shrugged. There were too many people around for him to bring himself to apologize. Besides, what did he have to worry about from a Primary kid.

"I can't help it if your mom's a bag," he shrugged, grinning at the older boys.

Unfortunately for Nick, Paul's father taught him how to box when he was five years old. Before anyone saw him move, a straight right jab shot out and planted itself onto the older boy's nose, knocking his head back against the roll-up kitchen window with a rattling clank. Three more times his quick right hand shot out. Paul spoke as he struck, each punch punctuating his words and meaning. "My mother's," SMACK! "not," SMACK! "a bag." SMACK!

Nick collapsed in a heap against the wall, holding his bloody nose with both hands. The other boys stood stupefied and wide-eyed at the fury unleashed from what looked like just another Primary kid.

Tracy saw the commotion from the far end of the hall by the

Bishop's office just as the fight ended. Grabbing Paul by the elbow, she took him to the other side of the hallway, well aware of silent stares around her. He relaxed when he felt her touch and let her lead him, though he was still breathing hard from his rage. He was almost as tall as she was and could easily have pulled away.

"It wasn't Paul's fault, Sister Fuller," said one of the young teachers standing by Nick. "He was just taking up for you."

Tears welled in Tracy's eyes as she looked at her angry boy. Matt, too, had started to cry when the fight began. The people in the crowded hall had stepped back. It wasn't every day they saw a fight in the chapel. Skip and a very pregnant Kate Garret walked around the corner hand in hand and seeing the boy on the ground, stepped up to make sure everything was all right.

Little Matt choked off a sob and glared at the downed boy, fighting the urge to kick him. "He called my mama a bag so Paul punched him in the beak."

Skip nodded. He saw the boy wasn't badly injured and chuckled to himself. He knew Nick Winthrop to be a smart alec and general pain in the neck. Leaning over, he whispered into the injured boy's ear. "If you'd said that about my mama, they would have had to peel me off of you." With a smile to the surrounding crowd he patted the bully on the head and stood up.

"You don't have to take up for me, Paul," Tracy shook her head back and forth slowly. "I'm a grown woman. It doesn't matter what some stupid kid calls me."

Paul pressed his eyes hard with the palms of his hands. He felt sick to his stomach seeing his mother cry. "Sorry I'm making you sad." He stared down at the rust-colored carpet. Tracy pulled him close and hugged him and little Matt both in silence.

"Are you in a big hurry to get home?" Skip asked, standing beside them and holding Kate's hand again.

Tracy shook her head. Her eyes held a look of exhausted sadness that made Kate give Skip's hand a do-something' squeeze.

So he smiled his wide, easy smile at Tracy while he gave Kate an I'll-do-my-best, Sweetheart squeeze back. He loved being married to someone he could communicate with without a whole gob of words.

"Kate has some teacher stuff to talk over with you and I thought Paul and I might go for a little walk— if you don't have to rush right off."

Tracy nodded and looked down at Paul who shrugged, still staring at the floor. "That would be fine," she said.

Paul normally liked to spend time with Skip or Terry, especially when they went fishing or camping. This time, though, he was afraid Skip might get on him about the fight. He didn't look mad but there was no telling with this particular grown-up. Sometimes when they were camping the man would go a whole hour without saying a word. Paul had never know anyone besides Skip or Terry who could go so long without talking when they weren't mad.

The air outside the chapel was warm, with only the hint of a breeze. It had been a hot summer and from the looks of things it was going to be a late fall. The farmer who owned the alfalfa patch behind the church grounds was trying to squeeze a third cutting out of his crop and the sprinklers tittered and spurted, making the warm air smell clean. A trace of the cool mist drifted across the fence, hitting Skip and Paul in the face. "Just what you need to cool you off." Skip took off his hat to enjoy the breath of a shower.

"I'm cool enough, I guess." Paul had taken a small, vine maple sling shot from his pants pocket and was shooting small rocks as fast as he could find them, pinging them off the metal sprinkler pipe. His father had made it for him the week before he died.

"Anything you want to talk about?"

"Not really." Paul found a perfectly round rock the size of a glass marble and aimed at one of the spokes on the sprinkler wheel thirty feet away. The surgical tubing pushed the stone out with a satisfying whir. Half a moment later, the rock slammed into the thin spoke and zinged into the thick alfalfa. Skip raised an eyebrow and nodded approvingly at the accuracy.

Paul knelt down again and scratched through the grass for another piece of ammo. "I hate that I hurt my mom's feelings, you know."

Skip combed a hand through his hair. "I know it, and I'm certain she knows it too. Do you think you would have been so hard on that boy if your dad was still around?"

Paul shrugged. "Don't know. I guess I might have warned him first, but I doubt he would have listened to me."

Skip nodded. "I'd say you pegged that right. Some folks need a bit of convincing before they stop their bad behavior. This is just the gospel according to Garret, you understand, so don't you be quoting me, but I say if you don't have enough sauce to take up for your mother's good name, you don't have much sauce." He put his hand on the boy's shoulder. "The plain fact is your mom's worried about you. She fears you're growing up too fast with everything that's happened."

Paul let another stone fly with his slingshot. "I think my dad would have wanted me to take care of them."

"I'm sure he would. But I'm just as certain he'd want you to have some fun at the same time. Your mom would feel better if she could see you smile once in a while." Skip took a deep breath and looked down at the boy. "Look Paul, life's been pretty rough on you, I know. Your dad was my friend ... and I don't have many friends. I hated to see him go. But as time goes by you've got to see that life isn't all sad and sour things."

"I know it's not." The boy looked out at the sprinklers for a moment, thinking, then up at Skip. There were tears in his eyes. "Sometimes I just get so tired."

"You know what?" Skip said gently, taking the slingshot for a try with it himself. "You sound like a guy who could use a vacation." He sent a rock toward the sprinkler wheel and missed—but just barely. Then winking at Paul, he said. "I just might have an idea."

CHAPTER 4

Every time Leon Dahl watched a plane land on the glassy blue water of Ptarmigan Lake he expected to be killed—or at the very least hauled off to prison where he would only wish he was dead. But so far his plan had remained airtight. Everyone at the back country lodge thought he was Sam Jenkins from Anchorage. Few people pried too deeply into anyone's private life in the bush and it proved to be the perfect place to hide. There was a certain amount of going along to get along out here, and even if they suspected something might be fishy in your past, most people minded their own business. Leon was a chronic worrier but he was also a quick learner and fit in nicely as the lodge handyman and general helper. So far no one had even given him a sideways look. Of course they hadn't. Why should they? He hadn't spent any of the money. He worked hard and kept his nose clean. Besides, only one other person on earth knew of his plan.

Beautiful, jewel-eyed Masha, with her stark, platinum hair and pouty lips; his heart ached to think of being without her even for these few weeks. He trusted her with his life and indeed, in confiding in her that was just what he had done. The Petrov family of the Russian Mafia was not the sort of group that forgave people for stealing. Vasilii, the eldest of Viktor's nine sons, the one with the hideous diagonal scar across his nose, had never liked him anyway. Leon was sure the young man would jump at the opportunity to kill him even if he hadn't stolen their drug money. Leon was not Russian and to Vasilii, that meant he couldn't be trusted.

Dahl secured the mooring lines of the lake's newest arrival, a dark blue floatplane, to the wooden dock and chuckled to himself. Vasilii had been right about him all along. Of course that would just make things worse if they ever caught him. Old man Petrov had granted him the family trust over his son's objections. They'd probably smuggle him back to Russia and take care of him there where everyone could watch. No, death would not come quickly for him in that case. Leon shuddered at the thought of it.

When he'd come to Ptarmigan Lake the month before, Leon often dreamt of being caught by the Petrovs. After a few weeks, the dreams decreased but he still had them. With all the drugs he'd helped move and money he'd helped launder, the Russians weren't the only ones who wanted him. The police were after him as well. The whole operation came crashing down just after he stashed the money in a cozy little Bahamian bank. Most of the Petrovs were wanted too, but they had so many fictitious IDs they came and went from Russia under a different name every week.

The old German forger in Anchorage charged Leon two thousand dollars for his fake Sam Jenkins driver's license. It seemed expensive but he had plenty of money—or would have once his plan came together. All he had to do was stay underground for a couple of months and hide from the Petrovs and the law. It seemed to Leon that the whole world was after him. The Russians, the Feds, Interpol, the State of Alaska ... he even had some unpaid parking tickets the city of Anchorage was unlikely to ever forget.

Flipping the wet line from the back of the floats around a metal cleat on the dock, Leon flexed his shoulders. He was amazed at how strong he'd become with a few weeks' honest work in the outdoors. He wasn't a big man. In fact most people would call him short but that didn't matter to him. He was quick with his mind and capable enough with his hands. Masha said she liked his blonde hair and boyish looks. She was two inches taller at five eight or so, but was always careful to wear flats so as not to exaggerate the difference. Leon thought about growing a beard or even a mustache to change his appearance when he went on the run but found it next to impossible to coax up more than a few wayward sprouts. In the end he settled for dyeing his hair black, but his looks remained boyish.

Boyish or not, Leon Dahl was no weakling. Being short, he fought a lot growing up and knew how to brawl. He shied away from the drugs that were his stock in trade, preferring the money to the product. Lifting weights and watching what he ate kept his waist trim for Masha. Hard work and the clean mountain air made him feel even stronger. He was in the best shape he'd been in all his thirty-eight years. Feeling the muscles flex under his light grey flannel shirt, he drew a deep breath and rocked his strong neck from side to side. If Vasilii came alone he might even stand a chance of winning if a fight came about.

Leon helped an older couple, wearing brand-new fishing gear, out of the Beaver and onto the floating dock while Roger Morely, the portly lodge owner welcomed them to his remote home. The pilot handed out the luggage and fishing rods. Leon hefted the heavy bags easily. It was always this way. When the planes landed, he panicked. When no Petrovs or police emerged, he regained his composure and a little bravado to go with it.

Rolling his shoulders with the luggage, Leon fell in behind the couple and their host. "Let them come," he thought to himself. "Petrovs or the cops—I don't care ..." Then, before they made it off the floating dock, he heard the whine of another plane banking in on a final approach to the lake. An icy chill ran up his spine and suddenly, the luggage was much heavier.

CHAPTER 5

"You know I'd go if could." Skip sat behind his desk holding a framed photograph of his new horse. "I'm afraid Kate would have my hide tanned if I went fishing in Alaska with the baby so close."

Terry sat on the edge of the wooden desk swinging his legs back and forth. "Sure, you'd be glad to go if you could drive or take a boat. Seems to me the last time you and I escorted an outlaw to Seattle you got so green around the gills I thought you might get sick on your fancy new boots."

Garret raised his hand. "Don't talk about that. Even dreams about flying make me sick. I'd rather be in a running gun battle than get on an airplane."

"Anyway," Terry said, mercifully letting his partner off the hook. "I don't mind going. I can testify as to what a bad idea it would be to let Mordekai Yeager make bond and there's no sense in both of us going for that. Besides, I have friends in Alaska."

"I hope it helps Paul to get away some," Skip said putting the photo back on his desk next to two others of Kate and Belle. A good horse, a good dog and a good wife. In a few weeks he'd have a good son. In Skip Garret's estimation, everything else in life was just gravy.

"Tracy says he's excited about it. I think he wishes you were going, though. I guess he's a little scared of me." Terry stood up and scowled at his friend, giving him the meanest look he could muster. With his forehead wrinkled up to the top of his shiny bald head and his deep squinting eyes, it looked mean enough to quiet a barking dog.

Skip grinned. "I don't know why anyone would be scared of you, partner. You're as softhearted as a kitten—completely nonviolent."

"Sure I am, but I'll bet there aren't many folks at church who'd send their kids out to the Alaska wilderness to go fishing with me."

"Their loss then," said Sherry Prather, the pretty, redheaded clerk. Though not a deputy, she was smart and capable and the two men valued her opinion. For the first six months she worked with them she'd been scared of Terry herself, but over time she'd relaxed enough around him to joke some. "They just don't know you like we do." She handed Terry a pink slip of paper with a phone message on it. "Thompson wants you to give him a call in Helena about the Yeager thing. He says he needs a leave slip if you're taking time off after the hearing. He also asked if you would E-mail him your itinerary, so if you'll give it to me I'll do it."

Terry took a deep breath. It was common knowledge around the district that Terry McGreggor considered himself a heck of a lot better gunfighter than a computer operator. No matter how hard he tried, he couldn't seem to get the hang of the cursed things. As full of grace and finesse as he was shooting or fighting, it all left him the moment he sat down in front of a computer. It was as if machines hated him and usually he got some kind of error message in the first two minutes of work. Christina had a computer at home, and even young Zane sat down with his father on several occasions to try and explain it. It was a hard on Terry to have his eight-year-old get exasperated with him.

McGreggor was a good enough worker that the Marshal still let him get by without too much work on the computer. He kept the only electric typewriter remaining in the district at his desk and pecked away at it when he needed to write a report. The whole E-mail thing seemed unnatural to him. It was too much like a pager. People could get hold of you too fast. Luckily, Sherry looked out for him in that department and sent his E-mail for him. She was making noises lately about wanting to go to the Academy and though they supported her wishes, both men dreaded the day they would lose such a capable helper.

Terry scratched out his itinerary on the pad at Skip's desk and handed it to Sherry.

"This looks like tough duty," she said looking at the paper. "A day in Anchorage for court and four days at the Dog Lake Lodge fishing. You think you might need me to come along in case you need to E-mail somebody?"

Terry's brow wrinkled in pretend horror. "You don't think they'll have computers out there do you?"

"I don't know, they might," Sherry smiled. "You might need me."

"Forget that, my dear," Skip said. "I need you here. Terry needs to worry a heck of a lot more about grizzly bears than electronics." He looked down at the picture of his young wife, then back up at his friend. Port's words about them getting into some kind of trouble haunted him, especially with Terry going off to the Great White North. Skip Garret was not a person to sit around and fret over things, but it stood to reason that if something was going to happen, either he or Terry would have to handle it without the other's help.

CHAPTER 6

Pulling the laminated checklist from the door compartment of the Cessna 180 floatplane, Kit Tipton began her before-landing checks. She was less than five minutes away and had already received permission from the Fairbanks tower to put down on the pond.

Her real name was Karen Irene Tipton. She'd grown up in the bush of Northcentral Alaska with a Scottish father and an Athabascan mother. Her father, also a pilot, coined the name Kit when she was only two because her boundless energy reminded him of a baby fox. The name Karen had been her mother's idea anyway. He'd never really cared for it since he had a girlfriend by the same name back in high school who he felt did him wrong.

All Kit ever wanted to do was follow on her father's wings and fly. As a child, she begged to go on every flight with him and by the time she was sixteen she had more hours behind the yoke than the skinny school-taught instructor she took lessons from in Fairbanks. She always managed to be in the right place at the right time and by age twenty she had three back-country rescues under her belt. Her mother had lost one brother to an airplane crash and was furious her only daughter had taken up the trade.

"If anything ever happened to you, your mother would never forgive me," her father said shortly after she got her commercial license. "She always did hold me personally responsible for your career choice."

"I'm me, Dad." She gave him a peck on the cheek. "Not you."

"No," he said with the proudest, but most forlorn look she had ever seen. "You're not me—but you're my fault."

From that day on, when Kit flew, she carried a laminated index card clipped to the yoke of her aircraft. Written in her flowery penmanship it said, "If this plane crashes, it not my father's fault." But she wasn't the one who crashed.

Now she toyed absentmindedly with the edge of the card and turned the yoke of her canary- yellow Cessna for the base leg of her approach to the Fairbanks float pond. She adjusted the flaps to slow down her plane and double-checked to see that both tanks were sending fuel to the engine. Her thumb slid across the laminated card to a photo of a tall, serene- looking man wearing the dress red tunic of a Royal Canadian Mounted Policeman.

"Let's see Mac," she said to the photo, the sound of her voice broadcasting back to her from the wire mike on her own headset. She often chatted with herself on long fights, sometimes about the business of flying the plane, most of the time about her boyfriend and hero, R.C.M.P. Constable Mackenzie Roberson. "I've got these two passengers to pick up—a kid and a copper like you out for a fishing trip, and some fancy kind of marmalade for Roger Morley's finicky guests over at Ptarmigan. Then it's a short slip across the border to Dawson to see you, my sweetie." She kissed her index finger, then touched it to the face on the photograph.

Final approach and landing required all Kit's attention and she tried to put Mac out of her mind. She felt he was getting pretty close to popping the question, though, and her thoughts drifted back to him as soon as her pontoons settled comfortably on the water. "A copper like you," she said again under her breath." If he's the talkative sort maybe I can quiz him about what married life would be like with one of you policeman types."

As much exhilaration as Kit felt when she flew, she was always happy to get back to earth again and stretch her legs. "We cheated death once again, old girl," she said to her little yellow Cessna while she secured the mooring lines from the slender aluminum pontoons to the small wooden dock of her rented slip. That done, she straightened up to her full five-foot-three inch height and arching her back, tried to work out some of the kinks from the two-hour flight.

Stew Swensen, a beefy, blond pilot about twice her age had the engine cowling open on his Cessna Turbo 206 and was grousing about how much oil it had been using. The 206 was beautiful; powder blue with white accents and half again as big as Kit's 180. It made a far more serviceable charter plane but with the extra size came an extra heavy price tag that Kit couldn't afford. Besides, she thought of her little yellow bird as more of a friend than an airplane.

"You know what they say, Stew," she hollered across the narrow inlet to the other pilot. "If they aren't leaking oil then they're out of oil."

Swensen smiled and wiped his hands on the front of a grimy pair of overalls that had it not been for the grease, would have been bleached almost white from hours in all types of weather working on his plane.

"You are right about that my girl, and I guess I should go get her some more to drink," he said, pitching a socket wrench back into the tool bag on his dock. "You going out again today?"

"Yeah." She rolled her shoulders, letting them warm through her plaid long-sleeved shirt in the afternoon sun. "I've got to get out to Roger Morely's at Ptarmigan. He's got some rich guests with more money than brains who will just die if they don't have some bitter orange marmalade with their crumpets in the morning. Roger asked me to bring out a case of the stuff—along with some crumpets. I'm gassing up there anyway."

Swensen smiled and thought of the tiny quirks of some of the passengers he'd taken to the bush. Usually they had to do with things people thought they couldn't live without for three or four days; like fuzzy gorilla slippers, teddy bears, or bitter orange marmalade to go with their crumpets. One guy actually brought his pet tennis racket and spent most of his fishing vacation backhanding rocks into the river.

"You need help loading?"

"No thanks," Kit nodded toward the back of her plane. "I already did it. It wasn't much. I'm just waiting for two passengers who're going past Roger's up to Dog Lake."

"Be careful then," he said and walked up the grassy hill to where his beat-up red truck sat, leaking more oil than his airplane.

Kit turned her attention back to the Cessna and got a small stepladder out of the plywood shed where she kept her gear. She'd add a few more gallons of fuel—just to be safe. Filling up the wing tanks from her wobbly ladder required all her effort and concentration and she didn't hear the two men come up behind her.

"Please excuse me, ma'am," The thick Slavic voice startled her so much she almost dropped a gas cap into the drink. A young, dark-haired man caught the metal cap in a bony hand and offered it back up to her. He might have been said to have a pleasant face had it not been for the three-inch scar running from under his left eye across the bridge of his nose. Once Kit replaced the cap he helped her down onto the bobbing pontoon, and then the dock.

"You don't sound like I thought you would Mr. McGreggor," Kit said, offering her free hand to the man to shake. Her other hand still held the fuel nozzle. "Or are you McGreggor?" She studied the other man. He was much taller, with deep eyes and a dark bristly mustache that grew wild and untamed beneath a great hawks-bill nose. The taller man had a ruddy completion and looked as though he was accustomed to the out of doors; like he might even survive in the Alaska bush for a few days. He had a meanness in his eyes Kit had seen in some of Mac's friends on the force. Maybe he was the policeman.

The tall man said nothing but shook his head, deferring to the younger one who smiled again—a plastic, almost painted-on, lips-only smile. His accent was thick and guttural and he held his head sideways when he spoke as if it pained him to explain himself. "No, neither I nor he is named McGreggor. The gentleman over there by his pickup truck said you were going to Ptarmigan Lake." The man eyed the 180. "We would like to buy two tickets to this lake, please."

"Sorry," Kit said, moving the stepladder to the other wing so she could finish fueling. "I've already got passengers booked. They should be along any minute."

The smile disappeared and both men moved a step closer. "You do not understand. It is very important we get to this lake. We will be happy to double your normal fee, for we are expected at this place today."

Kit stepped down from the ladder, her fuel nozzle in hand. The taller Russian had moved closer too, but still said nothing. The corners of his wide mouth twisted in a cruel smile under a bushy black mustache. Towering above Kit like an adult over a small child, he stood less than two feet away from her. The one with the scar on his nose was much shorter but he had the same ugly, condescending twist to his smile. He did all the talking and it was apparent he was the leader of the two.

With her back to the water, Kit had nowhere to go. Growing up in the bush, far from most other human beings except her family had made Kit's sense of personal space more guarded than most and the way these men crowded in didn't scare her as much as it made her angry. Scar Nose was now close enough she could smell the sausage he'd had for breakfast on his breath. It was obvious he was used to getting his way where women were concerned. His gestures became more animated and his voice rose an octave as he explained again his urgent need to get to Ptarmigan Lake. As he spoke, Kit tilted the nozzle to her fuel barrel ever so slightly, letting it drip on the young Russian's loose khaki pants. Neither man watched her hands but stared intently into her eyes in an effort to intimidate her. After all, she was only a woman.

By the time Scar Nose felt the cool breeze of gasoline evaporating from his pant leg, Kit already had the Zippo in her left hand and the top flipped open. One flick of her thumb and a warm yellow flame danced on the wick of the silver lighter. She held her hand back a few inches so fumes from the gas wouldn't light unless she wanted them to.

"I'm so sorry," Kit said with a flat smile and the dark, native eyes she inherited from her mother. "It looks like I've spilled a little fuel on you. It's very flammable, you know, I think maybe you should step back."

The taller Russian unfolded his arms and looked at his boss for an order. Kit let the lighter swing forward a little and even the hint of a smile disappeared from her face.

"I see," Scar Nose said, nodding his companion away and taking a step back himself. "I believe you have misunderstood us. We mean you no harm."

"I understand you just fine," Kit said, stepping forward a bit so she wasn't on the edge of the dock. "I think you'd better leave."

The young Russian opened both hands in protest. "But we ..."

"You must be Miss Tipton," a soft but penetrating voice came from the end of the dock behind the two Russians. A bald man with a dark, drooping mustache and piercing green eyes stood by a boy wearing a maroon baseball cap with CTR printed above the bill. "If you are, I believe we have you booked out to Dog Lake Lodge." He set the two small bags he carried on the dock and studied the situation.

Both Russians' heads snapped around and Kit waved, flipping the lid closed on her lighter with a click causing the younger Russian to turn and see if she had set him on fire.

"That's me. You're at the right place." The Russians excused themselves and shuffled past Terry and Paul without making eye contact.

Terry set his bag on the dock and turned to watch them leave. "Forgive me for asking, Miss Tipton, but are you okay? It looked to me like those guys were bothering you."

Kit shrugged and hung the gas nozzle on a hook beside her fuel barrel so she could shake hands with her two passengers. "No problem," she said, gripping Terry's hand firmly. "They just thought I could give them a ride and I told them I already had you booked. By the way, my friends call me Kit.

"The name's Terry McGreggor. It's a pleasure to meet you, Kit." Terry prodded Paul forward. "This is Paul Fuller. We've just spent two days in Anchorage and he's ready to see the real Alaska now."

Paul took off his ball cap and shook Kit's hand. He had a strong grip for a boy and Kit told him so. He blushed and returned the hat to his head so he could hide under the bill.

"All right then," Kit said, clapping her hands together. "If you two want to hand me your gear, we'll get this show on the road. Mind the float though. It's a tad on the slippery side."

CHAPTER 7

"Ever flown in a bush plane before?" Kit asked Paul while she stowed the black plastic tubes holding their fishing rods.

"No ma'am," he said looking over his shoulder at Terry for reassurance. He was smart enough to see that the whole trip was for him and it all made him a little nervous. As torn up as his life was, he deeply respected Terry and wanted to please him almost as much as he had wanted to please his own father.

"Well then," Kit threw her head to get her bangs out of her eyes, her long black hair shimmering in the sunlight like one of his mother's velvety curtains. "If Mr. McGreggor doesn't mind we'll make you honorary copilot and let him sit in back."

Terry smiled and tipped his black, flat-brimmed hat. "Suits me fine. But please, call me Terry."

Kit showed them both how to buckle their harness-type safety belts and reached across Paul to make sure his door was properly secured. The cabin was cramped at best, and Paul thought how pleasant she smelled. Not at all like any woman he'd ever been around. The girls he knew at school mostly smelled of shampoo or perfume and his mom smelled like fabric softener—but the pilot, she smelled different. Paul adjusted the bill of his ball cap so he could look over at her without being too conspicuous and took a deep breath. She smelled like the breeze blowing through the trees in his front yard.

He watched her closely while she went through her preflight routine, checking things off a list as she went. From the side it was easier to see she had a slightly bent, Indian nose and high, smiling cheeks. Paul's dad had a big photo book about different tribes with a picture of an Indian princess in it. He couldn't remember which tribe it was but thought it must have been the same tribe as this pilot's because they were both pretty. He wondered if it would be rude to ask what kind of Indian she was but then decided against it.

Back in the third grade, Paul had had a crush on his teacher, Mrs. Whitehead, but she was nothing like this Kit Tipton. By the time the tower gave clearance to takeoff and Kit had turned the plane into the wind, Paul decided that she was the most mysteriously beautiful woman he had ever met.

Even with the headsets the roar of the engine during takeoff was deafening inside the little plane. Kit adjusted the throttle to get the power she needed and aimed into the wind. The airplane shook and groaned as it bounced along on the rippling water. The propeller threw back a spray of mist; the plane seemed to come up on the water a little and the bouncing disappeared. Kit pulled back on the yoke and the next second they jumped from the water, trailing tie lines and water droplets from the pontoons. The plane stopped groaning and the engine noise quieted some.

After she got clearance from the tower to turn on her course, she turned to Paul and spoke into the little microphone attached to her headset.

"Are you ready for a crash course in flying?"

Paul smiled at her little joke and said "Yes," but didn't have his microphone in the right place. Terry helped him adjust it. When it was right he said, "Sure," and was surprised to hear his own voice come over his earpiece.

Kit was patient and didn't seem to mind a bit that he looked like an idiot who didn't even know how to use a headset.

"Flying's easy," she said. "Put your hands on your yoke so you can feel what I'm doing."

Paul did, lightly as if the yoke was hot.

"It won't hurt you. Grab hold of it. There, that's good. Now, look out the window at the river below us."

Paul leaned forward, holding the yoke. "Yes, ma'am."

Kit raised an eyebrow. "Kit. My friends call me Kit."

"Okay."

"Good. Now, that's the Chena. Watch what happens to it when I pull back on the controls." She did and the nose pitched up sharply. "Now we push in." The nose dipped. "See what happened to the river?"

"Yes," Paul said, hanging on every word.

"See, flying's a cinch. You pull back, the rivers get smaller; you push in, the rivers get bigger. Now, you know pretty much all there is to know about keeping an airplane in the air."

Paul nodded. "Because we climbed and then came down, right?"

"Exactly." She took her hands off the yoke. "Now you try."

Paul did, less scared now to touch the controls. He liked this woman. In a world that seemed so fragile to him, she was ... unbreakable.

Though it was mid-August, some of the trees below had already been kissed by frost and their leaves were beginning to turn yellow. A short time after they left Fairbanks the houses and roads were replaced by hundreds of lakes and winding streams. Paul saw his first caribou about thirty minutes into the flight; a lone bull with tall yellow antlers so heavy they made its head tilt back and its nose point toward the plane. Being from Montana, Paul had seen plenty of moose and even a black bear but he'd never seen a caribou before and it made him feel like he was living in the pages of one of his father's National Geographic magazines.

The animal ran through the brush and stubby trees, paralleling the bank of a willow-choked stream. Probably scared of the plane, Paul thought with his cap pushed back and his face pushed up against the window.

Kit brought the plane around so they could get a better look at the water. "See all that red and green in the water?"

"What is it? Moss?"

"Fish," Terry said into his mouthpiece. He'd seen them before but was still impressed by the sheer number of them.

"Righteo," Kit said, flying the curve of the streambed only a hundred feet off the deck. The water was alive with teeming red bodies at the elbow of each bend, where the water was slower, fish crowded into a solid mass of red the color of gaudy lipstick. "Salmon swim hundreds of miles from the ocean to lay their eggs in the same stream they were born in. And ..." Kit pointed to a huge brown lump in the middle of the water below them. "Where there are salmon there are usually bears."

Paul craned his neck to keep the bear in sight as the plane flew overhead, afraid the noise would scare it away. The black bear he'd seen in Montana had hightailed it into the woods as soon as they knew anyone was watching them.

But this bear wasn't moving. Kit brought the Cessna around in a slow turn with the bear in the center so Paul could keep it in sight. "Looks like a big boar," she said. "He'll just sit there fat and happy eating salmon and laying on lard for the winter. Normally the inland bears don't get as big as the ones by the coast, but those that live by salmon streams get enough food to get close to their size."

The grizzly looked up at the plane but continued to chew on the salmon it held between two massive front paws. Every few seconds it would lean into the water and catch another fish in its mouth letting a half-eaten one float away in the current. "This time of year, if there are enough fish they just eat the eggs and eyes because they are the most nutritious."

Paul was mesmerized by the size of the bear. "He knows we're up here and doesn't even run away."

Terry smiled from the back seat. "We're in his territory now and he's bigger than all of us put together. There's not much reason for him to run."

"I've seen them watch planes fly over and get so interested they keep looking until they fall on their backs. Sometimes it's comical watching them from the air but I try to steer clear of them on the ground. I think we're both happier that way."

"Have you ever hunted them?" Paul asked, still looking at the bear while Kit made her final pass and returned to course.

"With my father."

"It's a pretty big one." Paul shook his head at the thought of being on the ground with such a monster. "Does your dad still hunt them?"

"Nope. He died in a plane crash a few years back." Kit looked straight ahead.

Paul breathed out hard at the information. He thought, "I bet you miss him," but he didn't say it. Instead he looked out the window at the rusty yellow landscape below.

After a while the flat gave way to jumbled hills and then mountains. They hadn't flown over another human being for at least an hour but the land was far from deserted. It seemed that every pothole of a lake had a bear, a moose, or at the very least a pair of snow-white trumpeter swans decorating the surface or banks.

"Has anyone ever crashed down there and had to survive, do you think?" Paul asked after an almost reverent few minutes of silence.

"Sure, every now and then." Kit gave him a toothy, reassuring smile. "But don't worry, I'm not expecting us to crash."

"Doesn't every plane up here have to carry survival gear?" Terry asked, knowing the answer but wanting Paul to know, too.

Kit nodded. "That's right. The FAA has a whole list of stuff from food to a firearm all pilots have to keep in their aircraft. Mine is in a duffle behind the rear seats. I call it Kit's Kit and it's got enough stuff in it for four people to survive for two weeks without hunting. With a little ingenuity and as long as game is plentiful a person could survive the winter."

"That would be cool, living off the land down there," Paul said in a hushed tone, his nose still glued to the side window.

"It would be a lot of work, I know that." Kit pointed out her left window. "I grew up on my parent's homestead about a hundred miles that way. We lived off what meat we hunted and the supplies my father brought in from the nearest settlement forty miles away. Every year my mother planted a little garden but the moose got more of it than we did."

Terry laughed to himself. "I'd love living like that, but I'm afraid my bride wouldn't take to it very well."

"It's hard living but I think it was worth it. My mom's Athabascan, so she didn't mind at all."

Paul knew she was an Indian princess. "Do you speak Athabascan?"

Kit shrugged. "Just the 'mother words,' like come here, sit down, be quiet, and the stuff she would say when she got angry."

"Cool." Paul looked down at a huge bull moose browsing in willows next to a small pond. "You are lucky to get to live in a place like this."

"I think I am. I didn't even know what a TV was until I was thirteen and went to my aunt's house in Fairbanks." She winked at Paul who was imagining himself leading such a life. "I had a four-dog team I used to run a trapline when I was not much older than you. It was pretty cool I guess but it was an awful lot of work. The bush is great place to be if you are prepared but it's also very unforgiving."

Kit pointed to a small black box the size of a pill case low on the console between herself and Paul. "If we were to go down that's our insurance."

"An ELT?" Terry asked. He'd flown on military aircraft more times than he could count and knew the systems fairly well.

Paul leaned forward to get a better look at the little box. It had a small half-covered silver toggle switch and an unlit red LED.

"It's our Emergency Locator Transmitter." Kit flipped the silver switch and Paul's headphones were immediately assaulted with a pulsing, electronic whine. After a second or two she switched it off again. "I can turn it on here, or if we hit the ground hard there's an automatic switch in the back. Other planes pick up the signal and report it. With a little math and a map they can figure out where we are."

"Won't they be checking on us now since you turned it on?" Paul asked.

"Nope, pilots up here test their equipment periodically. It takes a little longer than that before anybody starts to worry."

Paul looked out the window at a land that at once seemed frightening and inviting. "Well, I hope we don't have to use it."

"You've got my vote there," Terry said into his mike.

"Mine too, gentlemen. Mine too." But Kit wasn't worried. The weather was perfect and she had a date with Mackenzie Roberson. There was no reason this flight would be different than the dozen other that week.

CHAPTER 8

By the time the hum of Kit's yellow Cessna disappeared from the Fairbanks float pond, Vasilii Petrov was seething on the shore. None of the Petrovs were known for their patience. The huge scar across Vasilii's nose was a result of a temper tantrum by his sister, Estar during a family disagreement. His father laughed and complimented the girl on her skills with a razor. Vasilii had been only fourteen at the time, but if Estar hadn't been family he would have taken a pistol and killed her. Now he laughed about it. The scar did make him look intimidating and the girls seemed to like it. He'd even thanked her for making his face look frightening to match his heart. Family deserved every consideration.

Vasilii had thought the foolish girl Masha might be hard to persuade into giving up her boyfriend. In the end, she had been so frightened by his looks that he didn't even need to hit her to find out what she knew. He hit her anyway; as punishment for her part in betraying the Family. He would have killed her, but his father forbade it as long as she cooperated.

In a family as large as the Petrovs there was little need to give much trust to outsiders. The old man even had to approve prospective sons-and daughters-in-law. Business secrets stayed in the family. On the rare occasion that someone abused the trust of the family retaliation was quick and cruel. Usually carried out by Vasilii.

And now the American had betrayed the family. Vasilii correctly assumed that his father had sent him to collect Dahl because the old man knew of his particular anger at the American. Once Vasilii found out where Dahl had hidden the money—two million dollars—he didn't intend to bring back much of the traitor. But first he had to catch him.

Young Petrov stomped his foot on the gravel shore like an angry child. "We must find another way to this Ptarmigan Lake before Dahl finds out we are coming."

Adrik smiled and toyed with a bushy mustache matching wild black eyebrows. If the girl had only cooperated they could have made it to the lake without causing a scene. The plan had been to get Dahl, take the girl's plane once they had collected him, and get out of the country before the authorities in civilization had caught on. But she hadn't cooperated, and they needed another plan. Across the finger inlet of the float pond the old man who had been working on the 206 when they arrived puttered around in a small metal building.

"Can you fly such a plane?" Vasilii looked out at the large Cessna. It seemed so much bigger than the yellow one.

Adrik nodded, studying the plane himself. "It has been a long time but I am sure I can do it. The flying will be no problem, but the floats I will be rusty on."

"But you can do it?" Vasilii grew more impatient with each passing second.

"Yes, I'm sure I can."

Petrov smiled a crooked grin. When it came down to it, there was not much of anything Adrik couldn't do. Ten years older than Vasilii, Adrik acted as a sort of uncle to the young man, though he always remembered he was an employee and not really family.

"All right then, let us go take care of it while the old man is still in the shed and out of sight. With any luck at all no one will find the body until our job is done."

CHAPTER 9

Sometimes the weather can be too calm when you're trying to land a floatplane. Ptarmigan Lake looked like an emerald green mirror as Kit made a low pass over the lodge to try and judge which way to land. The glass-calm water could wreak havoc on a pilot's depth perception but Kit set down without a bump, sending up a fine plume of spray. Turning the plane toward the floating dock running from a sprawling, honey-colored log building, Kit turned back to Terry. "Just one quick stop to drop some fancy orange marmalade off to Roger Morely, who owns the place. He lets me stash fuel here so as soon as I gas up and drop the package off we'll be on our way to Dog Lake." She nudged Paul on the arm. "I heard the fish are biting at empty hooks out there."

Morely met the plane at the end of the dock and introduced Sam Jenkins, a helper Kit didn't recognize. Jenkins, a short, fit-looking man with dirty blond hair secured the mooring while Roger helped Paul and Kit out of the plane.

"Hello, Kit my dear," Morely said, kissing her on the cheek. He was a kindly man with a healthy belly and enough of a jowl to remind Kit of her favorite uncle. "I really appreciate you bringing by the marmalade. These folks are the fussiest I ever saw." Terry took the box of jam from the back seat and handed it to Paul. He was still rummaging through his bag for a map of the Dog Lake area. Roger took the box immediately and started for the lodge.

"Sorry I can't stay and chat but to tell you the truth the Gatefields are about to run me ragged."

"No problem at all," Kit said, already getting the small stepladder to add a little fuel. "I'd do anything for you, Rog." Morely was almost to the end of the dock when Kit remembered the Russians. Jenkins helped her with the gas cans.

"Oh Roger," Kit took a step up the dock. "I almost forgot. I'm sorry I couldn't give those Russians a ride. They were too pushy for me, though, so don't recommend me to them anymore."

Morley half turned and started to explain that he didn't know what she was talking about but he saw Mr. Gatefield, his impatient guest, eyeing him out the lodge window. "Quite all right Kit. No problem at all. Don't worry about it." It would take far too much time to find out who she meant and it really didn't matter. He expected no other guests, particularly pushy Russians.

At first mention of the Russians, Sam-Leon Dahl-Jenkins nearly dropped a metal av-gas can into the lake. His legs turned into wet rags and he had to grab a strut on the Cessna's wing to keep his feet. Watching his boss disappear into lodge, he let his mind go into overdrive. He had to think. If the Petrovs had tried to get a ride with Kit, they would be right behind her. He knew the way Vasilii operated. The young gangster might try the nicer, less attention-grabbing method of renting a plane to start with, but if that didn't work, someone was going to end up hurt … or dead. One way or another the Petrovs got what they wanted.

In five seconds Leon's gut went from a gripping, crippling fear to the kind of stampeding panic that causes frightened buffalo to run headlong off the edge of a cliff. He had to get away from Petrov and he didn't care who got in his way. He couldn't figure out how they had discovered his plan. Masha wouldn't have told him … but she must have; she was the only one who knew. The thought of her betrayal added a sickening mix of rage and sadness to his belly and he let out a low, guttural moan that caused both Kit and Paul to turn and look at him.

Jerking a black Sig Sauer autopistol from his waistband, he shoved Paul, who was standing more in the passenger door than out into the back seat. He needed the boy to make the pilot do as she was told. Backing away two steps so he had a view of both the boy and Kit, he pointed the pistol at her and ordered her into the plane.

"Get us out of here. Now … or I'll start with the boy." Dahl was beyond thinking and his words came out of his twisted mouth as a continuation of the fearful growl that first escaped him a few moments before. Kit hesitated, surprised to be staring at a gun. "I don't have anything to lose. Get in the plane." Dahl let the barrel swing toward the plane fully expecting to shoot the boy to convince her. But she ran without another word and jumped in the pilot's seat. The fact that he could exercise some small amount of control helped Dahl's condition to some degree but he swallowed back panic when he thought of what would happen if he didn't move fast.

Leon kept the gun leveled at Paul and climbed in beside him. "You," he shouted to Terry who stood empty-handed on the dock. "Push us out." He punctuated his words by waving the pistol in the boy's face.

The deputy kept his face passive, his eyes locked on the madman. "Happy to, friend, no reason to hurt the boy." Using the passenger side wing, Terry pushed the little plane away from the dock. At the last possible moment, he jumped on the float and into the front seat beside the pilot. On Dahl's orders, Kit had already started the engine, and she turned the plane out toward the middle of Ptarmigan Lake. "Who invited you?" Dahl barked. "Get out now or …"

Terry didn't want the man to make any promises he might think he had to keep. He searched his brain trying to remember the name Morely used when he introduced his helper. "Hold on there, Jenkins. I can't very well let you fly off with my friend, now can I?" Terry knew he was liable to get shot, but at the moment death seemed a lot more desirable that facing Tracy Fuller without her son.

"Where to?" Kit said, breathing deeply and trying to keep from looking behind her.

Dahl shook his head to clear it. It had all happened so fast he didn't really have a plan, but if he'd had one, it sure wouldn't have included a mean-looking bald guy in the front seat of his getaway vehicle. The wires in his brain seemed to be crossed and a million voices screamed inside his head, making it difficult to think, let alone speak coherently. He nodded east. Then pointed with the gun so Kit could see it. "That way."

Kit started to put on her headset but Dahl shook his head. "No!"

he snapped, motioning with the pistol for her to take it off. "We can live without them. I want to hear everything that's going on."

Terry looked over at Kit. Keeping his hands low, he held his open palm down against the seat, telling her to remain calm. Paul squished against the side of the plane trying to make himself as small and inconspicuous as possible.

When she reached 3,000 feet Kit took a deep breath and looked back at her captor. "Are you going to tell us what this is all about, Mr. Jenkins?"

Leon stared at her, blinking his eyes as if he was trying to figure out who she was. He had been thinking about his beloved Masha, wondering how she could betray him. "What?"

Kit gripped the yoke, exasperated. "Why are you doing this to us?"

Leon nodded, coming back to the present situation. It didn't matter if he told them now. "My name's not Jenkins, it's Dahl, Leon Dahl. Those Russians you are talking about want to kill me." His eyes were bloodshot and glazed. "Or worse. They think I have some of their money."

"Do you?" Terry asked in a rough, power-filled voice from the front seat. His own pistol was packed in the bag a few inches behind the kidnapper's head. The man sat directly behind him, which made it almost impossible for Terry to do anything but bide his time.

Dahl looked Terry hard in the eye, then shoved the gun barrel cruelly into Pauls ribs. "Shut up, all of you. I need to think and I sure don't need to explain myself to you. Let's all try and remember who has the gun here."

Kit's jaw set in grim fury. The throb of anger pounding in her ears all but muted the drone of the plane. At Leon's screaming insistence she had the engine at redline, urging the 180 as fast as it could go dragging the floats through the air. She was burning fuel rapidly and had no idea where she was going. From the dazed look of terror on Leon's face, neither did he. This man seemed the type to run off a cliff if he got spooked and Kit had no desire to go over with him.

"Where do you want me to point us?" She looked back into Leon's wide eyes. They had gone yellow and bloodshot in a matter of seconds. "If we stay on this heading going this fast we'll run out of gas in about forty-five minutes." Kit paused for a moment to let the words sink in. Leon darted a glance at the fuel gauges but said nothing. When it was apparent he wasn't going to answer her, the young pilot settled down in her seat and concentrated on the line of craggy mountains ahead of her. She was headed roughly east, across the border and into the Yukon Territory.

"There are no gas stations up here, you know," she said a moment later, becoming more annoyed with this stupid man with each passing minute. "If you want to die, the door latch is by your right hand, you're welcome to go ahead and jump. As for the rest of us, we're heading for Spruce Lake to get fuel."

Dahl kept the gun pointed at Paul's belly but shot a glance behind him out the window. "You'd better not be taking me to any major airport." He shook his head, attempting to clear it. The constant whine of the engine noise inside the cramped cabin suffocated him. A cloying fear gripped his throat and made rational thought impossible. "Just let me think." He tapped the barrel of the pistol—still aimed at Paul—against his open palm.

"I think you need to be flying lower in case they have radar or something."

Kit looked at the altimeter and shook her head. They were cruising at 3,000 feet. "It's safer up here Leon, believe me. When you're flying, altitude above you is worthless."

"Shut up and get us lower," he snapped. Sweat dripped steadily from the man's forehead and into his eyes, forcing him to blink from the sting. The muscles in his jaw twitched under tight skin.

"You do exactly what I say, or I'll shoot the boy, I swear it." He cuffed the boy on top of the head with his free hand.

Paul's eyes widened and he sat back tight against his tiny seat, not knowing what to do. He looked to Terry for guidance.

Terry gave a slight reassuring nod and quick wink. He had been mainly silent since the hijacking, biding his time and waiting for an opportunity to act rather than react. He didn't waste time wishing he had his Glock. He didn't have it, and that was that. If he had to make a move it would be with his hands. The confines of the small cabin made any movement risky. Though the plane wasn't pressurized, there were plenty of things a bullet could damage that were required to keep it in the air. Not to mention the fact that someone was very likely to catch a round. But, this threatening business had to be stopped, one way or another before things got worse. Keeping his hands quiet on top of his head, actually a pretty good place for a martial artist, Terry kept his voice matter-of-fact. The simple way he spoke without any outward emotion brought a chill to the cabin and even the droning engine seemed to grow quieter.

"If you strike the boy again, you'll force me to take action. Somebody will get hurt even if you don't intend for it to happen … and that somebody may be you." Terry relaxed the muscles in his arms, poised to act at the slightest movement from Dahl. The man still had his pistol pointed at Paul's chest. Though Terry felt fairly certain he didn't want to shoot, this whole mess proved he was irrational and irrational people did things they didn't intend to do.

The bottom of the plane suddenly seemed to fall away as Kit pushed the yoke forward against the console. Leon felt his stomach rise to his throat but kept the gun on target. "What are you trying to do?"

"Exactly what you told me to—I'm going lower. I don't want either of you two macho guys shooting holes in my airplane."

Leon nodded smugly at his small victory. "Well, do it slower."

Kit complied and slowed her descent, finally leveling off at 500 feet above the terrain.

Terry watched the man's reflection in the side window and considered his options. The wiry deputy was certain enough of his abilities he was sure it would all be over in the blink of an eye if he could only get one good distraction. So far, though Leon had spit and screamed like a wildcat, he hadn't taken his eye off Kit or the gun off Paul long enough for Terry to make a move.

The radio in the dash of the 180 squawked to life. "Yellow Cessna, yellow Cessna." The crackling voice clicked with a Slavic accent. "Leon, are you there?"

The static message brought even more sweat to Dahl's face and his eyes darted around the cabin. It was impossible to tell if he was about to shoot or jump out of the plane.

"I see you, Leon." The voice came back again. "You are yet a speck on the horizon, but I still see you. There is no place to run … Do you hear me, my old friend?"

Without a word Leon sent three quick rounds into the lighted display of the radio, then brought the pistol back to bear on Paul. Acrid smoke filled the cabin and a crackling spray of sparks showered from the radio panel. Warning buzzers to various electronic gadgets began to squeal adding to the cabin pandemonium.

"You idiot," Kit spat. She switched off various pieces of nonessential equipment. With Leon still watching her, she took a chance and flicked the tiny switch that activated the ELT. If Leon noticed, he didn't say anything. "You may have killed us all," Kit said barely loud enough for him to hear.

The little plane yawed badly back and forth and the heavy grey smoke grew thicker. "You must have hit an oil line." Kit reached down between the seats and cut off the fuel lines to the engine. There was a sputter while she trimmed out the propeller, then a whir. "We're going down pretty soon guys. I can't risk a fire in the engine."

Paul pressed his nose against the small window to his left. He'd said nothing since the ordeal started, for fear of getting shot. Now, with a prospect of a crash it didn't seem to matter. "There's a lake below us. It looks sort of small. Do you think it's big enough to land on?"

Kit shrugged and brought the plane around in a slow bank. Even with the warning buzzers whining the cabin seemed strangely quiet without the drone of the engine. "Its going to have to be. My options are pretty limited dragging these floats." Leon sat and stared out the windshield, the reality of what he had done dawning on him while the plane sank toward the jagged rocks and spruce tops below. They were trying to land on a lake so small that even from four hundred feet it looked to be not much more than an overgrown puddle.

They were approaching the lake from the southwest without much wind. Kit guessed it to be about three hundred feet long and not quite as wide. Even if everything went textbook she was still likely to end up on the opposite shoreline before this was all over. Looking over her shoulder and banking the plane as sharply as she dared without losing too much altitude, Kit turned to Terry. "Everybody make sure you're strapped in … and pray if you're the praying type."

The small lake grew larger before their eyes as Kit struggled to maintain her best glide path with sluggish controls. Just as she was over the last of the trees surrounding the lake, she pulled back gently on the yoke almost willing her little plane out of the sky. The stall-warning buzzers went off when she was still 25 feet above the water and the plane began to jump in the unsteady air. Gritting her teeth, she held back on the yoke, the far shore looming large in the windscreen. Causing the plane to slip and lose altitude, she'd done all she could apart from praying and thought she might have it made … until she saw the beaver.

The animal made daily trips across the lake, believing birch trees growing on the south side were far superior to the ones growing by his lodge. Unfortunately for the Cessna—and the beaver—it had chosen a particularly large limb to drag back across the lake and exactly this time to do the dragging. The plane was still going fifty knots when the left pontoon hit the swimming beaver, then the log. Bouncing back into the air as if it hit a trampoline, the right wing dipped, its tip driving more than two feet into the dark-blue water. All forward motion was stopped as if they had hit a brick wall and the 180 flipped around on the wing with a grinding crunch of twisted metal. The passengers were all thrown into their lapbelts.

To Kit everything moved in slow motion. Leon's arms flailed so much with the gun that for a split second Kit thought he might accidentally shoot her. The plane came to rest on its back with Kit suspended upside down by her belt. Once she realized she was still alive, Kit immediately began to shout orders. Leon unfastened his safety belt and disappeared out the open passenger door into the dark, rushing water. Paul hung dazed in his belt with frigid water gurgling in around him with a sputtering hiss. Wanting to optimize his chances if Dahl made a mistake, Terry had neglected to fasten his harness. Limp and unconscious, a huge gash on the back of his head, he lay crumpled on the roof of the plane in the rapidly gathering water.

"I can't do this alone, Paul," Kit said above the rushing tide. Her voice was strangely calm. "I'm going to need your help to get him out of here."

The boy nodded, pushing while Kit pulled and got Terry's limp body maneuvered out the open door and dragged him to the surface.

CHAPTER 10

Adrik Illya Ivanovich turned the heavy plane into a sharp bank high over the lake, keeping the wing tip of the crashed 180 in the center of his circle. Vasilii screamed at him to move in closer, pounding on the padded dashboard with the flat of his hand. For all his yelling and pounding Petrov couldn't fly a plane and Adrik wasn't about to get himself killed. His years in Afghanistan had honed the patience he was born with and taught him through many close calls that it was better to ease up to a place than to fly directly in and get ambushed. For all he knew, as incompetent as Dahl was, he might get off a lucky shot.

"There he is, I see him." Petrov's voice rose an octave when he got his quarry in sight. "Land this plane. Land it now." He pounded the dash again and looked at Adrik. "Why are we still in the air? I have business down there."

Adrik was used to such ranting, and he continued his circle. "The lake is too small for us to take off again even if we could land. Besides that, the yellow plane is right where we would need to set down. We will have to find another place near here."

Below, Dahl stood drenched to the skin looking up at the aircraft, his pistol hanging limply by his side. He seemed mesmerized by the slow circles. Adrik had seen the behavior before. Petrov had such a psychological hold on Dahl, his brain shut down when the Russian was nearby. He would pose no threat to the plane. Adrik came in a low pass and watched the

Indian girl and the boy drag the bald man onto the gravel beach. The girl had something else in her hand and he strained to make it out as they flew directly overhead. He chuckled to himself when he saw what it was. She must have hit a swimming beaver when she landed and now brought the lifeless body with her to the shore; to eat later in case they needed food, no doubt. She was a quick thinker and would be a formidable opponent. The tall Russian nodded happily at the thought. They needed to catch Dahl because he would lead them to the money, but he would be too easy. There was no enjoyment in fighting an idiot. Pursuing the smart Indian girl would be great sport and after what she'd done with the petrol at the dock, Petrov wouldn't mind taking the extra time after they took care of the money matter with Dahl. Finances always took priority—even over revenge.

Seeing Dahl so close sent a rattling rage though Vasilii Petrov and he pounded his head against the plexiglass of the side window so hard Adrik thought it might break. His eyes bulged from his head and spit flew from his lips with every word. "Get us on the ground now!" he fumed, bouncing in his seat like a spoiled two-year-old who didn't get his way.

"I will look for another body of water," Adrik said coolly, still thinking about how much he would enjoy stalking the girl. She seemed such intelligent prey. He brought the plane around for another low pass. She was busy tending to the bald man who was bleeding badly from a wound in his head. Adrik smiled. He had been right about her. She paid little attention to the airplane buzzing overhead: it couldn't land there. It was no threat and she wasted no time on it.

"I don't care where we go, just get us down quickly so I can deal with this." Petrov's voice calmed some but he still bounced with each word.

Dahl on the other hand still stood in a drug-like stupor staring white-faced and slack jawed at the sky.

CHAPTER 11

Once the plane was out of sight Leon shivered—as much from the cold as from fear. Though the sun was still up, it skipped low across the horizon and didn't offer much warmth. After effects of adrenaline from the crash and the fifty-five-degree breeze blowing off the lake made for a deadly chill. Like everyone else, Leon was soaked to the bone but he refused to allow a fire.

Terry sat slumped against a spruce snag on the gravel shore where the long yellow rays of sun did their best to warm him. Kit bandaged his arm as best she could with the bandanna she found in his back pocket. Paul sat with him, holding a piece of damp T-shirt to the back of his friend's head, in an effort to stop the bleeding. Terry had definitely taken the brunt of it during the wreck. The luggage strap behind him had snapped and let the cargo slam into the back of his head. He lapsed in and out of consciousness and Kit suspected a serious head injury.

While swimming ashore Kit had run into the body of the dead beaver that helped flip the plane. Thinking it might be the only thing they'd have to eat for a while she'd brought it with her and it now lay gutted at Terry's feet.

"Look," said Kit, wringing out he tail of her sopping shirt and standing to face Dahl. "Those guys chasing you are at least ten miles away. I'm telling you, I know this country and there is no place around any closer than that for them to land. Especially with my plane clogging up the lake like it is."

Leon didn't speak. Shaking his head he played the pistol back and forth from Terry to Kit as if trying to decide which one to shoot.

"What I'm saying is we still have some time." Kit's voice trembled. She had to concentrate to keep her teeth from chattering. "We all need a fire to dry off and he needs medical supplies." She nodded her head toward Terry whose lips were already turning blue from the chill. "He may die unless we get a fire and a first-aid kit."

"We're not havin' a fire so shut up about it. Where are you gonna get a first-aid kit out here?" Dahl's voice was quiet as if he were deep in thought. His eyes still searched the horizon for signs of Petrov, but the barrel of the ugly black pistol remained pointed at Kit's belly.

At least now he was talking to her.

"From the plane." She pushed a dripping lock of black hair out of her dark eyes with a shivering hand and pointed off shore to the exposed wing jutting from the dark water. "I'll probably die of hypothermia if we don't start a fire, but I have to go down for it. Whether we stay with the plane or not, we'll need food. There are MREs on board that won't have been hurt by the water."

"We've got the beaver."

Kit threw her head back in exasperation. "We'll need more than one beaver to keep us alive."

Dahl thought for a moment, then nodded slowly, though his face remained unconvinced. She was right, he would need food to get away from Petrov and better for her to get soaked again getting it than him. He couldn't remember being so cold even in the middle of winter.

"Go on then," he finally said motioning toward the water with the tip of his gun.

Kit walked up the shore to where Paul knelt beside Terry. She squatted next to them and patted Paul on the back of his soggy wool shirt. Leon still studied the horizon and had temporarily taken his eyes off them.

"Take care of him a few more minutes, Paul," she whispered through chattering teeth. "I have to go back to the plane and get some food and medicine for Terry."

Paul nodded, too chilled and scared to say anything.

Kit knelt closer to Terry and felt his forehead with the back of her hand. His right eye flickered open at her touch and she jumped at the intensity of his look. She turned to see if Dahl had noticed but he was still staring at the sky.

"I think my arm's broken, but I'm not hurt quite as bad as I'm making out to be."

Kit looked at the blood-soaked bandanna on the back of the man's head. "I think you're hurt worse than you're making out."

Terry started to speak but caught the long shadow of Dahl making his way toward them on the gravel beach.

"If you're going, get to it. I'm not staying here much longer. If you knew what was good for you, you wouldn't want to either. That Russian won't be satisfied with just killing me. He'll kill the rest of you just for the sport of it." Dahl looked at the direction in which Vasilii's plane had disappeared and his whole body was taken with such a fierce shaking that he could hardly control the pistol in his hand. Embarrassed that Kit had seen his fear, Leon slapped the girl hard with the back of his free hand. She staggered from the blow but kept her feet. Grabbing her by the shirt collar the man heaved her into the frigid water.

"Get moving ...now!" His eyes blazed yellow like those of a cornered animal.

The bank dropped off quickly and in four steps Kit floundered in water up to her hips. She gasped at the initial shock but her body was so cold the water soon seemed warmer than the air. Committing herself to the bone-chilling, life-draining blue of the lake, Kit leaned into the water and swam toward her Cessna's bent wing waving to her from the surface twenty yards away. Already, waves of exhaustion tugged at her senses and she knew if she didn't get back and get a fire going quickly all would be lost. She reached the plane in a few strokes but had to grab an exposed float support to catch her breath. Dahl stood shaking his head on the beach. When he saw her gasping for air he turned away, as if he'd given up on her survival.

Kit's eyes felt extremely heavy and the short swim had used up what little energy she had left after the crash. The water lapping at the bobbing float rocked her gently and she wanted desperately to drift off to sleep. But she had a plan and the thought of the plan alone was enough to drive her forward. Taking four deep breaths, she kicked her feet up over her head, using a twisted wing strut to pull herself under. With a splash not much bigger than a feeding trout, she disappeared and left nothing but a series of widening rings on the surface of the dark water.

The exposed wing had torn almost completely loose and once underwater she found the rest of the plane floated on its back like a dead fish, with the propeller about four feet below the surface. She almost cried when she found the door latch stuck on the pilot's side and for a moment thought she would have to try her luck on the side with the torn wing. She was running out of air fast and swimming to the other side of the plane seemed an impossible task. She knew if she ever went to the surface she wouldn't be able to come down again.

Working her fingers up along the door frame and wedging her feet against the metal body she found the latch was not stuck at all and the door was already open about an inch. She felt the door give and heard the sound of groaning metal over the throb in the back of her head. Squirming through the darkness into the cabin of the little plane, Kit reached above her head toward what was supposed to be the floor and felt what she was hoping for—an air pocket.

She'd been banking on the fact that some air would be trapped and had already decided that if there wasn't any she would rather die with her plane than go up and face the chill and foolishness of Dahl. The pocket was little more than six inches deep and she had to twist her neck sideways to get what little air there was. Electrical shorts caused when the instruments hit the water had filled the space with stale smoke, but it was air and Kit took it gratefully. It wasn't much and it wouldn't last long, but hopefully it wouldn't have to for what she had in mind.

In flight the cabin of the 180 was cramped at best but that turned out to be a blessing while Kit looked for the survival gear. She took a breath and submerged again searching by feel for the nylon duffle bag. On her second trip under she realized she had been kneeling on it behind the headrest of the starboard passenger seat. Returning to her tiny pocket of air, she hung the bag over one of the rudder pedals so it wouldn't float away and get lost.

Kit squinted her eyes in the dark water and tried hard to focus. There was still one more thing to do and she didn't know if she still had enough brain power left to get it done. It would require a certain amount of manual dexterity and thinking to accomplish—and she was sleepy, so sleepy she didn't think she could push herself under again, let alone do what she knew had to be done.

CHAPTER 12

Belle, the blue heeler, liked to rest her head on her man's thigh while he drove. It had been a warm day so Skip had the window open and tipped his silver-belly hat back to enjoy the evening air. Things at the office had been mercifully quiet since Terry had gone. With Kate so close to her due date, Skip hated to be away from her any more than he absolutely had to. She'd been over at the McGreggors' all afternoon and he'd found himself wondering about her well being when he should have been attending to the business at hand. Earlier, Brick, the new gelding, had quickly noticed and nearly dumped him on his head for his inattention.

Skip didn't like to admit it to himself, but when Brenda left him she'd hardened a little piece of his heart. His job had a tendency to make him a bit pessimistic about people in general and Brenda had reinforced that feeling when it came to women in particular. But day by day Kate Beebe tenderized him from the inside out. He still had no trouble getting his point across to the bandits at work, but his new wife had softened him—there was no doubt about that. He'd noticed even his animals responded better to him lately, which was saying a lot because they always seemed eager to please. There just seemed to be an extra bit of happiness in Belle's groan when he scratched her behind the ears; an extra lilt in the horse's gait.

Lost in his soft thoughts and the wind swirling around the cab of his pickup, Skip nearly drove into the ditch when he heard a voice next to him in the dim light of evening.

"Why, hello Brother Garret." Rockwell sat on the other side of Belle, a grey felt hat in his hands, his long hair tied back in two silver braids. "You sure do look happy. You catch an outlaw or two today?"

Skip straightened out the steering wheel and checked the rearview mirror to make sure he hadn't forced anyone off the road. "Good grief, Port, you shouldn't come up on me like that. I could have killed us … me. Trucks aren't like horses. They don't steer themselves very well."

"Sorry." Port shrugged off the chiding. "What do you hear from that partner of yours?"

"Nothing, why?"

Port's face looked grave. His eyebrows furrowed. "I don't know. I just heard some more talk about rough times. Haven't been able to put my finger on it, though. I was sort of hoping to get more information from you. We postmortal beings aren't as omnipotent as you might think. I still have to do a little detective work." Rockwell stared out the window and shook his head in thought. "I wonder how young Paul is doing."

"You think something's wrong?" Skip had put both hands on the wheel at Port's arrival and Belle nuzzled his elbow with her nose to get more petting.

"I don't know, but I aim to find out. What I do know is this, I'm prompting you, doggone it, so you best feel prompted!"

When Skip looked back, Rockwell was gone. Terry's house was only a few miles away and he would be there easily in fifteen minutes. He stared at the cell phone in his truck. As a rule Skip steered clear of the things if he could; they detracted from his cowboy spirit. Most news could wait and he never had much to say on any kind of phone. He'd only put it in the pickup so Kate could get in touch with him if the truck broke down.

Over Belle's objections, he stopped scratching her and picked up the handset, dialing in the McGreggor's number. Christina picked up after two rings.

"Hello."

"Hey my dear. It's Skip. Is my child-bride still there?"

"Sure is. Don't even come get her," Christina said. "We've decided to have a slumber party. Think you can live without her for one night?"

Kate giggled in the background. Skip shook his head even though he was on the phone. "Not a chance, Chris. I'm having trouble breathing right now we've been apart for so long. I'm only fifteen minutes away and I couldn't wait to talk to her."

"Okay, Romeo. You're starting to lose that tough-guy image you know. Hang on a sec."

"Say Chris, before you go, what do you hear from that husband of yours?" Skip tried to sound nonchalant. He was fishing for information and hoped she didn't notice the strain in his voice.

"Not a thing since they left Fairbanks. He said he'd call me if he could, but the lodge only has a radiophone so who can tell. Why, you need him to call you?"

"Nope, just wondering how Paul was doing." Skip could hear the edge in his own voice and knew if he talked long enough Christina would hear it, too. He needed to change the subject. Though he tried to make sure Christina stayed calm, he couldn't get rid of the gnawing in the back of his own mind. "So, where's that wife of mine? I'm starting to get brain damage here."

CHAPTER 13

The rifle was exactly where she thought it would be and Kit was able to retrieve it on her first try. Her fingers felt like they were wooden dowels with no joints and the slippery canvas bag was difficult to get unzipped in the cramped cabin. When she did get the case open, she had to be careful not to drop either of the two pieces of the weapon. Hanging the small sack of ammunition on the rudder pedal with the survival gear, she tried to fit the rifle together. With her neck cramping from trying to get air, she had to do it all by feel, under water. Very little oxygen was left in the small pocket of air and Kit could feel herself getting dizzy. Finally, after a bit of a struggle, she felt the two pieces click into place with a hollow, but comforting snap.

It was a simple over-and-under combo gun chambered for .308 Winchester in the top barrel and 12-gauge shotgun in the lower. Kit's father had given it to her when she started flying the back country and it made a perfect survival gun for the bush.

With great effort to keep focused on what she was doing, Kit thumbed open the barrels and reached in the bag of ammo. Cradling the rifle in the crook of her arm she knelt next to the front passenger seat and searched in the small cotton flour sack.

Making a mental note to herself to keep shotgun and rifle ammo separate in the future, she found one shell for each chamber and loaded the weapon. It click shut with another resounding snap. Kit suddenly felt better at the thought that she might be able to get warm in a very few minutes.

Taking one more deep breath of what was now mostly smoke and carbon dioxide, Kit said good-bye to her little yellow Cessna. Grabbing the waterlogged bag of survival gear in one hand and the rifle in the other, she kicked her way out of the plane. The bag caught once, but a good tug brought it along and she rose as quietly as she could on the away side of the far float. It took all her willpower not to cry out when she reached air, but afraid Dahl would hear her she stayed just beneath the surface. With only her face above water she sucked air like a bottom-feeding fish. Her short shivering breaths kicking up tiny ripples of cold blue water; she let her ears come up and strained to hear Dahl's voice above the swooshing throb that had taken over the back of her head.

He was talking to the boy, telling him to stand and get ready to go. "She's drowned by now," Kit heard him say. "Nobody can survive under water for that long. Tough luck kid, no food or medicine for your daddy here."

"He's not my dad—he's my friend," Paul said as Kit slid under the water and kicked toward shore. She worked her way diagonally away from the plane, well away from where Leon would expect her to come up. At least that's what she hoped she was doing. Her lungs burned, but she swam on, dragging the heavy bag and rifle beside her, a few feet below the surface. As her nose scraped the gravel bottom of the shoreline she ran out of steam. Letting the bag slide off her left arm, she took the rifle in both hands and rose to her knees.

The water hit her just below the belt as she knelt. She would have liked to be on her feet but her legs were so shaky she didn't think she could make it without falling. Less than twenty feet separated her and Leon when she broke the surface.

Dahl heard the noise and spun in terror thinking Petrov had somehow snuck up and gotten the drop on him. What he saw scared him almost as badly as the Russian. Although he had no compunction about killing, Leon could not be said to have lightning reflexes, or even sound slow ones. When he saw the blue-faced girl, her black hair covered in silt, with the rifle pointed at him, he forgot that he also had a weapon and froze in place like a jackrabbit waiting for an owl to fly by.

As soon as the barrel cleared the water, Kit pointed it at Leon and pulled the trigger. Her body shook violently from the mere effort of staying on her knees and she felt in no position to bargain or bluff. No, she had to send a strong message all at once. If the message hit Mr. Dahl right between the eyes, that was his problem. If it didn't, she still had the shotgun barrel. The muscles in her cheeks twitched, trying in vain to warm themselves, and strings of dripping hair hung in a tangled black mat across her forehead and face.

The .308 round went low and kicked up a spray of gravel a few feet in front of its intended target.

"I'd put the gun down, Leon." Terry's voice came from the snag on the beach. There was still a shotgun round left and it was likely to do far more damage than the rifle, even if her aim was off a little. Kit wasn't sure she could even speak so she didn't try. Instead she concentrated on keeping her quaking arms pointing the weapon at Dahl.

Seeing the maw of the 12-gauge in the hands of a creature who already looked half dead, Leon took a deep breath and dropped the pistol onto the gravel next to his feet. Terry, rose up on one elbow and waited for Kit to give some direction. She was, after all, the one holding the gun. But she just stood in the water, seemingly trying to decide whether or not to shoot Dahl on general principles. When Paul started to retrieve the pistol, Terry shook his head.

"Step away from the gun, Leon, and get down on your face." Terry's voice was strained but calm.

Dahl half-raised his hands and looked over his shoulder. One person holding the gun and one giving orders … he was beginning to wish he hadn't given up his pistol.

"Now!" Kit bellowed, her voice rising loud and shaky like a demented scream from the bottom of the cold blue lake. "Get down now!" Tears streamed down her face and her shoulders heaved in uncontrollable jerks.

Fearing she might snap at any moment, Leon took three quick steps away from the pistol and scrambled smartly to the ground.

"Now," Terry whispered hoarsely to Paul. "Get the handgun and bring it to me." He patted the boy on his hand. "Be quick."

His head was splitting and the throbbing ache in his right arm made it difficult to see. He was sure he felt better than the poor girl looked and he feared she might drop the rifle before Paul could get the pistol out of Leon's reach.

Even after Terry had control of Dahl's weapon Kit stood staring down the barrel of the shotgun. Everything around her seemed so hazy. Waves of fatigue washed over her even worse than the cold. "Have you got him?" She heard herself ask. When Terry answered she was instantly flooded with warmth and relief. Acting on autopilot, she managed to drag the gun and soggy survival bag ashore before collapsing altogether.

The closest lake Adrik could find big enough to land on was twenty miles to the north of where Vasilii wanted to be and he was in a dark mood because of it. They pulled the plane up in a narrow slough where they could get out and stretch their legs. There were few trees and a steady breeze kept the bulk of the mosquitoes at bay. Adrik sat relaxed against a car-sized boulder, studying an aeronautical chart and trying to get his bearings. The plane, though mechanically sound and powerful was sadly lacking in navigational instruments—at least any the big Russian knew how to use. "I think we have crossed over into Canada somewhere." He studied the surrounding boggy landscape and the hazy green mountains in the distance, trying to match them to features on the map.

Petrov shrugged. Borders meant nothing to him. "I don't care where we are if it is not on top of Dahl. You should just fly me low over the lake and let me jump out into the water. Then I could do what my father expects me to do."

Adrik shook his head. He couldn't say what he was thinking. The truth was old man Petrov had sent Adrik along on this mission because he knew his son was hotheaded enough to come up with such a foolish idea. Adrik had seen many such brash young commanders in Afghanistan. Only they were not so quick to risk their own lives, preferring to send their troops into any sort of suicide mission. No, Vasilii was not like that. He was foolish and impatient, but he was much too impatient to be a coward.

"I do not think that would be a good plan," Adrik said to his young employer. "Dahl did not shoot when we flew over before, but I think if you jumped into the water he might come out of his trance and shoot you while you swam to shore."

Petrov nodded angrily, seeing that it was an imperfect plan. "Maybe you could drop me on the far side of the lake and I could circle through the trees. It would not matter if they know I am there. They are probably all chilled so badly they couldn't hit me if they did fire."

Adrik gave a you-are-the-boss shrug. "But then, you would be chilled as well when you did get to shore and the slowest I could get this plane is perhaps sixty knots—a little fast to jump out and hit the water. If you were knocked out there would be no one there to help you.

Vasilii sat on the ground and buried his face in his hands like a pouting child.

Adrik suggested an alternate plan. "Leon knows you will be coming for him so he will move. We should fly over them again and look for another place to land to the south. If he is moving we will at least see the direction they are going."

Petrov looked up, a half-smile on his strained face. "Perhaps we should shoot everyone except Dahl."

Adrik nodded, not liking the thought of shooting the Indian girl without a proper and fair chase. "Leon may have already done that."

Petrov gave a contemptuous laugh. "The fool doesn't have it in him." He looked out at the plane bobbing a few feet away on the emerald water. "Still, the woman should probably pay in person for dripping the petrol on my leg." The young Russian shook with anger at her insolence. "No, if Dahl has not shot her we won't do it from the air. She should have to pay in person for the way she treated me." He swatted at his face. "These mosquitoes are becoming unbearable. If we do not get back in the plane, there will be nothing left of me to kill anyone."

It was some time before Kit woke up. The sun was low on the horizon but it was late in summer and the sun still spent a lot of time riding the ridge before it finally dropped out of sight. It was difficult for her to judge what time it was. Paul had the fire going a few feet away and sat near it helping support Terry's injured arm. Every branch and willow nearby had some piece of clothing draped across it to dry by the fire and the air around the small camp hung heavy with the smell of wet wool. Kit found herself wrapped in a foil emergency blanket with two instant hand warmers placed strategically against her belly. Her whole body ached when she tried to move. Even with the warmers she felt clammy and chilled but the shaking had stopped and she could focus more on things going on around her.

"I had Paul take you down to your woollies so we could get you warm," Terry said from the other side of the fire. He chuckled a little when she peeked inside the space blanket. "I've never seen a boy so relieved as he was when he saw you had on thermals."

Paul blushed and put another piece of wood on the fire.

"Go ahead and laugh it up." Leon sat dejected, tied to the snag where Terry had been before. He was close enough to the fire to get a fair amount of heat, and steam rose from his soaked jeans and boots. "Yeah go ahead and laugh your fool heads off. You won't be laughing when Petrov and his stooge Adrik get here." Leon struggled against his bonds and his eyes burned with hate. Bits of spit flew from his mouth with each word. His face was drawn and his eyes dark and bloodshot. Fear gnawed at his gut; the same fear that causes a trapped animal to chew its own leg off to escape. He pounded his head against the stump behind him.

"You've got to listen to me," he whimpered. "I don't care if I go to jail for the rest of my life. You can't let them get to me. I ... I've seen what they do to people who cross them." Dahl's eyes glazed over. The thought of whatever he imagined was too powerful for him to put into words. His head lolled back and he stared into space in a dazed stupor.

Terry shook his head slowly in thought, studying the outlaw to take his mind off his pain. The tiniest movement made his vision blur and he had to squint to see clearly. Most of the bandages from the first-aid kit in the survival bag were on the back of Terry's head. He'd taken a couple of Ibuprofen and the pain in his arm had dimmed to a hollow ache.

"As much as I hate to say it," Terry said. "I think Leon's right about moving."

"And leave the plane you mean?" With Dahl quiet, Kit relaxed a degree and studied her bare toes as they warmed by the fire. She shook her head at the prospect of leaving. "I don't think that would be such a hot idea. If the ELT was working before we went down, the last location anyone will have on us is here—or near here at least."

Terry nodded. "True, but we're not sure it was working."

Paul stirred the fire with a long piece of spruce he intended to smack Dahl with if the man got loose. "My dad always said if you get lost you should stay put until someone finds you." He spoke timidly, never before questioning Terry on anything.

"And your dad was absolutely right. But we're not only lost. We are being hunted," Terry said. "Ordinarily I'd stick right here and wait for help, but from the way Leon is acting I think we're all in danger. The people in that plane know exactly where we are. If they come after us we're in a terrible position to defend ourselves."

Kit shook her head slowly at the fire, still unconvinced. "We still have the guns."

"That we do, and we may need them. I'm down and not much use in a hand-to-hand scrap. Paul here is a stout young lad and I don't doubt his courage—but he's never faced men as bad as these. You've shown yourself to be quite capable, but even you are completely worn out." Terry shrugged, then winced at the pain it caused him. "We could stay here and fight but the outlook for that isn't very promising. I've lived my whole life on strategy and I promise you the best strategy here is not to meet these people head-on. We need a place to hide out and heal some; we need a place to regroup and plan."

It was a long speech for Terry, who preferred to let Skip do most of the speech giving. Christina said that's why they made such a good team—Skip explained things and Terry backed him up with a "yup" and a stare.

Kit wiped a smudge of dirt from the corner of her eye. "What about our rescue? People will be looking for us soon. If we leave here they won't even know where to look."

"If we don't leave here, we'll be dead when they find us," Leon said from his spot on the other side of the flickering fire. He was taking a great interest in the turn of the conversation.

Terry turned his head with slow deliberation and pointed an open hand at the prisoner. He didn't particularly like the fact that they were arguing the same point. "You keep quiet. If I need information about the people chasing you I'll ask for it. Otherwise, not a word."

The effect was immediate. Terry's hard gaze shut Dahl up as completely as a gag.

"Okay then, say we do go. We'll have to take Leon with us?" Kit spat at the thought of saving a man who so easily could have killed them all.

"Correct."

"Won't that make it hard to keep him tied and let him walk at the same time."

"I've already thought of that," Terry said. " We can rig leg restraints of sorts out of the cord from your survival gear." He turned and looked directly at the prisoner. "I know it would affect the boy for life if he had to witness such a thing, but if you put us in jeopardy again I'll be forced to kill you without any discussion. Understand?"

The man nodded a trembling head.

"All right then," Kit said holding her hand up toward the sun hanging low on the horizon. "We've got about an hour till the sun drops out of sight and then another hour of dusk. After that maybe four or five hours of dark."

Terry worked his way to a standing position, willing away the sickening groan that swam low in his gut. The act made him dizzy and he clung to Paul's shoulder for support. In a few moments the feeling passed and he was able to stand on his own.

Suddenly, Dahl began to thrash at his bonds. His eyes darted wildly, back and forth across the sky. "I can hear them coming back," he blurted, immediately looking at Terry, afraid he would shoot him for the outburst.

Terry pulled the pistol from his belt with his left hand and scanned the sparse woods around the beach.

Kit held up a hand and told Dahl to be quiet. "It's a plane."

Paul nodded. "I hear it too. Maybe someone got the emergency signal."

"Maybe," Kit said softly, scanning the sky as the droning engine grew louder.

The 206 came in low on the first pass, not fifty feet above the trees. It was Petrov.

"I told you it was him," Dahl babbled, throwing his head back in a long, pitiful howl. "Mooove me! They'll shoot me out in the open like this."

The whoosh of wind over the wings was easy to hear, even with the roaring engine as the plane made a slow pass overhead.

Kit didn't mind Dahl thinking he would be shot at any moment but his blubbering got on her nerves. "Shut up, Leon," she snapped, watching the 206 fly a quarter mile, then do a slow rolling 180 for a return pass. "You said they need information from you. They want you alive until they get it."

When the plane came by again Vasilii Petrov's smirking face was pressed tight against the passenger window. He waved at Leon, who sat mesmerized, unable to tear his eyes away from the man who craved a pound of his flesh. Petrov mimicked the shape of a pistol with his thumb and forefinger and pointed it at Dahl. When the plane was directly overhead a two-liter, plastic pop bottle fell from the passenger window and landed with a hollow plop in the lake, a few feet from the shore. Paul fished it out and handed it to Kit. There was a note inside.

"We only want your prisoner," the note said in hastily scrawled script. *"Leave him tied here where he sits and all will be well with you. If you run with him, we make no promises."*

The 206's engine noise grew dimmer and it disappeared from view. Kit read the note aloud, watching Dahl's eyes grow wider with every word. Smiling, she held the note up to Terry. "This sounds like a good deal to me. There obviously aren't any lakes very close or they would have landed already. By the time they get back here to get Leon, we can have Paul out to safety and you to a doctor."

Leon jerked at the cord on his wrists. "You can't be serious!"

Terry pondered the idea for a minute, more to keep Leon guessing than to make any real decision. The decision had, after all, already been made. It was one thing to kill Dahl if he had to, but the man was now his prisoner and he couldn't very well leave him behind. Beyond the moral obligation, Terry felt the prospect of abandoning Dahl to the Russians would do irreversible damage to young Paul. While dragging him along was the more difficult road, for the time being there was little choice.

The air temperature hovered a hair above fifty when Kit judged everything dry enough to travel. A cool, dusky evening had crept in around them and a crisp breeze blew in off the lake. She took a blaze orange day pack out of the survival bag and started to take stock of the provisions.

Leon groaned when he saw her roll out the brightly colored bag. "That's just great. Why don't you set off a flare so Petrov will know where we are all the time?" The man's face was gaunt with fear and the words came out more whiny than cynical.

Kit fumed in annoyance. "That's usually the idea when you're lost. I didn't plan on having to hide after a plane crash."

Waving off any further conversation, she laid their meager supplies beside the day pack. What they had didn't amount to much, but Kit Tipton had grown up in the bush. She was used to making do with very little. What gear they had should keep them alive—if no other disaster dropped down on top of them.

Since she'd started to fly, Kit had always been careful to carry the appropriate survival gear. All the equipment required by Alaska and Canadian law had been stored neatly in the duffle when she left Fairbanks, but now the bag was almost empty. A large, jagged tear scared the end where Kit had dragged it against the damaged metal of the Cessna. All the food and much of the gear had fallen out in the plane. Some of it probably still floated in the airspace inside the cabin.

Apart from what they used to tie up Dahl, there was about thirty feet of parachute cord left. There was a large black-handled Buck knife in a scabbard which Kit slipped on her belt and a handful of shells for the combo gun. She laid them out carefully and counted them. Ten shells for the shotgun and eleven for the .308 plus one for each that were already in the gun. Leon's pistol still had seven rounds but there were no reloads. Terry's Glock was still in his bag on the plane. There were two plastic water bottles, a spool with about twenty yards of heavy fishing line, two fishing lures, two headnets, a green tube of military insect repellent, three foil blankets including the one Kit had already used, and a roll of fifty feet or so of thin wire Kit could use to twist into snares. The matches must have fallen out with the food but Kit always carried certain basics on her. She reached into the pocket of her wool pants and felt comforted when she found her Zippo lighter and magnesium fire starter and striker. Paul had used the lighter to start the fire earlier.

Terry had made a fair dint in the small first-aid kit, but there was still a bit of antibiotic ointment and aspirin. In the bottom of the plastic box holding Band-Aids was a small, handheld pencil flare. It had a pull striker which ignited the white-hot flame that burned for about four minutes. It was more of a fire starter than a signaling device but it could prove useful.

Paul had been watching the inventory with great interest. One part of him felt as if he were in the middle of a great adventure; part missed his mother very much. "We're not going to have much to eat, are we?"

"Not from the plane," Kit said and then thumped the roasted body of the dead beaver. "But we won't starve. I never liked beaver as a kid, but it will make okay survival rations. All of us are pretty much in shock, though, so we shouldn't eat too much at a time or we'll get sick." Kit remembered her dad's sled dogs nearly dying when they got into some spoiled beaver meat when she was a child. Even now the smell of the cooked animal made her nauseated. "Other than that, there is plenty of stuff around here to hunt."

"I feel like I'm the one being hunted," the boy said, swatting at his neck. "These mosquitoes are getting bad." Kit threw him one of the green net hoods. "Put this on your head and tuck your pant legs into your socks. The little punkies aren't as big as the skeeters but they have a way of finding any bare skin."

A great grey cloud of mosquitoes and no-see-ums had descended on the small group along with the dusk. Leon, whose hands were tied, was having the worst time of it and kept blowing hard to keep them off his face. A crop of growing pink welts on his cheeks and forehead was all he had to show for his efforts. Kit sighed and put the other netting over his head.

"I guess you and me will have to make do with repellent," she said to Terry. "There are only two head nets." She squirted out a handful of smelly white cream and handed the tube to Terry, who gratefully accepted. He was used to wearing a hat and his bald head provided a tempting smorgasbord for the insects.

Kit smeared the greasy cream on her neck and face. "It keeps mosquitoes at bay at least. I think the punkies like the taste of it."

Terry leaned on his spruce walking stick and looked down at his prisoner. "On your feet Leon." While Kit was going over their gear, Terry tied Dahl's feet so he had about two feet of cord connecting at each ankle. It was loose enough the prisoner could move around slowly, but restricted him from running. Dahl's hands were tied to another cord that wrapped around his waist.

Paul was eager to do something to help out and put the orange day pack over his shoulders. It was so light it almost felt empty. "Do you think they'll start looking for us pretty soon?"

Terry took a shallow breath to protect his aching ribs. "As soon as Skip figures we're not where we're supposed to be he'll hightail it up here pretty quick."

Kit brushed a lock of hair out of her eyes and swatted at a punkie while she was at it. "Who's Skip?"

"My partner." Terry turned on his walking stick to scan the dark line of trees along the beach.

Leon snorted at the idea of such devotion. "What makes you think he'll cut loose and come up to the Yukon because your plane has been missing a few hours?"

Terry stopped in his tracks and turned slowly toward Leon. "Because I would for him." He paused for a moment, breathing heavily and gathering his thoughts. Then he smiled and nodded toward the trees in front of him. "I'd like to have you up here by me Mr. Dahl. I believe I need to keep you squarely in my sights."

"There are some high mountains to the west of here," Kit said. "They may offer us some places to hide out once it gets bright again."

"Good idea," Terry said scratching his neck and shooing away the hovering cloud of bugs. "You lead out. I have to leave Skip a quick message. If I know him, he'll be riding in here on a borrowed horse in a day or two."

Terry took out his pocket knife and worked it open with his left hand. He found a suitable white birch noticeable from where they had built the fire and scratched out a short message in the chalky bark. Writing with his left hand made it difficult to get something readable, but he worked steadily and finished in a few minutes. The carving was easy to see and anyone looking for clues would be sure to notice it.

He stepped back to admire his handiwork, using Paul's shoulder for support. The boy studied the letters and numbers carved in three-inch blocks on the tree trunk. "What about the Russians?" Paul asked. He was beginning to feel more comfortable asking questions of the adults.

"Only Skip will be able to make out what I mean—he should know exactly which way to go."

Kit picked up a two-foot piece of sharpened birch sapling on which she'd skewered the roasted beaver and turned her back on the group. She needed to pick a route through the trees that would lead them to the mountains, so she left the business of guarding Leon to Terry and the boy. It was comforting to see the confidence the man had in this Skip of his. She hoped he was right. For her part, she was certain someone would be coming for her, too. The stout little Athabascan girl smiled at the dark, empty woods ahead of her. Like the U.S. Marshals, the Royal Canadian Mounted Police had a reputation for always getting their man. Knowing Constable Mackenzie Roberson the way she did, Kit knew he was the type to come for his girl as well.

CHAPTER 14

Skip was still sleeping soundly Friday morning when Kate rolled out of bed. Young Beau Garret had taken to waking up earlier in the morning than everyone else and his kicking caused her a considerable amount of heartburn, besides a lack of sleep. It was a little before six and the sun was just peeking over the green mountains west of the Garret place. Cool orange shadows crawled through the jack pine and across the corrals by the side yard, bathing Kate's blue cotton gown in rich color as she stood at the bedroom window. She rested a hand on top of her belly, trying to soothe the kicking baby. The way he bounced around inside her he was likely to be a basketball player. If he did, he'd come by it naturally. His father was a touch over six two and Kate stood five feet nine in her bare feet.

She looked over her shoulder at Skip and sighed softly. He lay peaceful with his mousy hair mussed and one corner of his thick mustache drooping toward his chin. He'd been out at the pens late the night before working the new bay gelding he got in Kallispel. Of course, Kate had been at the pens with him, but in her present condition Skip wouldn't let her near any of the animals except Belle. She felt fine, was actually past any morning sickness, and didn't feel quite as big as a beached whale. She accepted Skip's mothering, though, and resigned herself to watching from the top rail.

Anyway, it was a pleasure to watch him with the new horse—

the way he connected, almost read the animal's thoughts, anticipating movement before it happened. Watching him sit atop the powerful animal, moving it this way or that with nothing more than a cluck or a nudge of his knee, Kate thought how this quiet, almost awkward man had taken control of her life. Of course she gave him the control, just as the horse did. Skip did more than move things. He made them want to move. He possessed that quiet aw-shucks way that made women want to mother him and animals trust him completely.

She'd known he would ask for her hand long before he ever brought himself to do it. He'd been married before, after all, and good Mormon men his age didn't date the same girl for months unless they had a future in mind. There were two dates to the movies when she'd thought he brought a ring, but for one reason or another chickened out. Sometimes she found herself wondering how he'd proposed to Brenda, his first wife. But she always decided she didn't really want to know.

Then came the ward harvest festival. It was a hayride and bonfire held at Skip's place because he had the wagon and space for a ride. Kate helped him the entire week before, cleaning up the grounds and repainting the red barn. There'd been ample opportunity for him to pop the question many times while they were together. But something, something she couldn't put her finger on, made him hold back.

The air had been crisp that night, with only a faint breeze whispering through the Douglas fir that lined the driveway. The warmth of the bonfire and the feeling of Skip's calloused hand in hers made Kate feel heady. She could hardly remember any of the songs. There had been a good turnout and people milled about here and there, drinking hot cider and cocoa in the flickering, snapping light of a huge pine fire.

In the midst of the singing, Skip had gently led her out of the orange pool of light toward the barn. Her heart almost stopped as she walked beside him into the darkness.

"I need your help harnessing the mule and the dun mare," he had said with a quiet air of nonchalance.

Kate slumped. "You know I love you, Skip. I just want ..."

He put the tip of his finger to her lips. His look was soft and kind and something in his deep grey eyes calmed her unsettled heart and she followed him without another word.

A small bulb already burned in the barn and soft yellow light spilled out when Skip swung open the wooden side door. Fish, the stout red mule gave a half hearted haw when he saw the man, then resumed munching quietly on his hay. His torn right ear lopped over at the top like a hound.

"They're almost dressed." Skip pointed to the mule and buckskin mare in the adjoining stall. Both already wore heavy black leather collars and breeching. The flatbed wagon took up most of the alleyway in the barn. Earlier, Kate helped stack sweet-smelling bales of grass hay along the sides for people to sit on during the ride. Skip pointed at the stall with an open hand.

"If you'll get the mare and lead her around on this side, I'll grab Fish."

Kate knew her way around the barn and easily slid the homemade horseshoe latch open on the mare's stall. The horse followed her out, sighing contentedly in recognition. Skip had spent an hour bathing and grooming them, and Kate thought how good they smelled along with the freshly soaped harness leather. She led the horse around in front of the wagon and had already snapped in one of the tugs before she noticed the ring. It was tied with a small purple ribbon to a shiny brass D on top of the mare's harness.

Across the alleyway Skip stopped working and leaned happily across the mule's broad red back, resting his chin on his hands and looking at Kate. Fish, oblivious to the thick mood that had fallen over the barn, dropped his head and began to nibble at bits of hay on the floor. His lips made loud popping noises in the otherwise silent reverence of the moment.

She had to lean on the dun mare to keep from collapsing then and there, but somehow on spindly legs she floated or walked or something over to the mule and held up the sparkling ring. "Is this for me?" Her voice cracked despite her best efforts.

Skip had his hat back on the crown of his head and a big, toothy grin under his mustache. He reached across the mule's back and engulfed her slender hand in his. "If you want it."

Kate pursed her lips together and nodded, blinking to clear the blur that was forming in her eyes.

Skip squeezed her hand. "I think of you all the time, Katie. Heck, my days are just one long thought of you—punctuated by periods of concentrating on not getting shot."

Kate giggled, then sniffed. Skip handed her a red bandanna from his back pocket.

"I don't have much to offer you but this little place and me. I'd like for my home to be your home—my horses, your horses."

"Your porch, my porch?" Kate wiped her eyes with the bandanna.

"That too." His voice grew low and breathy. "Everything ... forever. If you will."

"Oh, of course I will, Skip," she said, sobbing and squeezing his hands. He took the ring and slipped it on her finger. His rough hands trembled slightly at the delicate act.

"I do have one request," Kate said, holding her arm out to admire the new ring.

Skip nodded giving a little shrug and opening his hands like a book across Fish's back. "Anything you say, sweetheart." His face glowed and he looked as if his big heart had swelled almost to bursting. "You name it."

"Well," Kate said, roughing the red hair under Fish's harness. "I need you to tell me this mule won't come between us again."

Skip let out a war whoop and swatted Fish on the rump with his hat. The mule squirted out from between them and he scooped Kate up in his arms. "Nothing," he had whispered that crisp autumn night. "No mule or horse or outlaw will ever come between me and my girl ...."

Now, almost a year later, his baby was kicking her guts out and giving her heartburn to boot. Leaning against the widow, she watched him sleep, his broad chest rising like a bellows under the quilts. She was about to go to the kitchen for an antacid when the phone chirped by the bed. The bedroom was small and she was able to get to it before Skip could roll over and answer it himself. She held the receiver in her hand for a moment before putting it to her ear, savoring the last few seconds of peaceful reminiscing. Kate Garret had been around Skip long enough to think of all calls before 6 A.M. as highly suspect.

And she was right. It was Russ Thompson, the supervisory deputy from Helena. Skip sat up on the edge of the bed and took the handset. Kate sat down next to him, leaning back on her hands.

"Glad I caught you at home." Thompson's voice was hesitant and had a hard edge to it.

Skip glanced up at the early-morning sunlight coming through the window and then at the bedside clock. "Russ, it's five fifty in the morning. Where else would I be?"

"Right. Well, I was wondering if you'd heard from McGreggor." The line went silent again. Thompson had been a capable deputy and was a good supervisor. Skip got along well with him, but found the way he beat around the subject annoying so early in the morning.

"No, no I haven't. Is there something I need to know?" Skip motioned for Kate to get him a pencil and paper from the desk at the far end of the room. This talk of Terry, taken together with Rockwell's recent visit made his stomach hurt.

"His plane is overdue at Dog Lake and nobody's heard from him or the pilot. They were last seen at another lodge about seventy miles from there called Ptarmigan Lake. Lodge owner's a man named Morley. Anyway, he says shortly after they landed to drop off some supplies his handyman disappeared with Terry, the boy and their female bush pilot named Kit Tipton."

"Was the handyman scheduled to leave?"

"Nope. Morley says he was real fond of his Russian girlfriend and kept snapshots of her all over his room. He left all his clothes and the pictures of his girl. Morely knew the guy as Sam Jenkins but shortly after he left another plane with two pushy Russians on board came in looking for somcone named Leon Dahl. They showed him a photo and it was the same guy."

"Did this Morely describe the Russians?"

"Yeah, one was big and mean and the other was little and mean. The little one had a diagonal scar across his nose." Thompson paused to catch his breath, and probably take a swig of the diet Pepsi he never seemed to be without. "Get this, I checked the warrant files on the computer and we hold a DEA warrant for a Leon Dahl on a multicount indictment for conspiracy and money-laundering charges."

"Conspiracy? So who else was involved with him?" Skip scribbled in the corner of his writing pad in an attempt to calm his nerves.

"That's where we get a bingo. Almost every one else is Russian, most of them named Petrov. Looks like a family business. One ..." Skip could hear paper rattling while Thompson checked his notes.

"Here it is," Thompson went on. "One of the Russians' name is Vasilii Petrov. He's supposed to be one of his father's top lieutenants and his passport photo shows a pretty substantial scar across his beak. This particular Petrov is also wanted on two drug-related murders in Alaska. Up to now everyone thought he'd gone back to Russia."

"This Dahl guy have any other history?" Skip asked, smiling at Kate who was beginning to look alarmed.

"Oh yeah. He's wanted by everyone from Anchorage P.D. to the Russian Militia. Mostly petty dope stuff. No assaults or anything. He always seems to be around dangerous sorts, though." Thompson took another swallow of diet Pepsi. "There's one more thing but I don't know if it means much yet. Canadian authorities picked up an emergency locator transmission around the time Terry's plane disappeared. They only had it for a few minutes and weren't able to get a good fix, but they believe it came from somewhere across the Alaska-Canadian border in the Yukon Territory."

"The Yukon? If anyone's done anything to Terry, I want to arrest them in the good old U.S. of A." Skip chewed on the drooping end of his long mustache and thought about Rockwell's warning. "I think I should go up there, boss. Either officially or on leave, I don't care which." Skip didn't look at Kate. He was pretty certain she wouldn't want him going off with the baby so close. Still, there was no choice.

"I knew you'd ask. Do me a favor, though." Russ proved he was a good supervisor by not saying no outright. Everyone in the district knew Skip and Terry were closer than brothers. Terry, having been in the military, was fairly easy to command as long as he respected his leader. Skip on the other hand, required more finesse. He was one of those cowboy types who might up and quit if something went against his personal code.

"McGreggor's wife doesn't know what's going on." Thompson continued. "I need you to check in on her and make sure everything's all right on that end. I'm not saying you can't go up there, but there's nothing for you to do now. The Yukon's a big place. When we get more information, then we'll make a decision. If you can do any good you'll be going officially."

Skip nodded, thinking about the unpleasant task of talking to Christina McGreggor. "Thank you, Russ."

"Okay then, I'll be in touch. You all right with this?"

"I'm fine." Skip said good-bye and hung up the phone. Tapping his pencil on the pad, he looked up at Kate. "Did you get that?"

"The gist of it. Do you think they're hurt?"

"Don't know," said Skip, already up and getting dressed. "I'm worried though. Terry's not where he's supposed to be and some pretty bad characters are coming to the surface of all this. I need to go talk to Christina and make sure she's all right."

Kate covered her mouth. "Poor Tracy. This is all too close to losing Wally."

Skip took a deep breath and nodded, standing up from the bed. "Yeah, this is going to be hard on her." He stepped in the bathroom and began brushing his teeth. "I'll go see Christina first and then check on Tracy." He spoke between brushing. "Would you mind doing me a favor and calling Sister Wulff. The Relief Society could maybe take by some meals or something."

"Well," Kate got her own toothbrush from the cup beside his. "I'll call Sister Wulff, but I'll do it from the truck phone because I'm going with you."

"Oh no, sweetie. That's a bad idea. You need to steer clear of such things right now."

"And just why is that, Brother Garret?" Kate spit into the sink.

They had never had what could be called an honest-to-goodness fight, but Skip learned shortly after they were married, when Kate called him Brother Garret, he was on the verge of practicing serious unrighteous dominion. He decided to take a little less firm position.

"Look, hon," he said, taking both her shoulders softly in his hands. "It'll be really bad. There'll be a lot of crying and tension. I don't want you to have to go through that in your present condition."

"Nonsense," she said kissing his chin. "I'll be useful over there. We're a team now, Skip. Remember—your horses my horses, your problems my problems."

Skip sighed. It was really no use and he felt stupid for ever thinking she wouldn't go. He looked at the determination in his young wife's face and shrugged. "You know I'd love to have you along," he said, thinking of something his father always used to say. *There are two theories about arguing with a woman—and both of them are wrong.*

"Much better, Brother Garret." Kate reached up and wiped a dab of toothpaste off his mustache with a washrag. "That's what I like to hear."

It was decided. Skip felt as though he was on a runaway horse, completely out of control.

CHAPTER 15

There is no good way to break bad news.

Christina McGreggor was in the middle of canning a big batch of applesauce and the house was filled with the cozy smell of cooked fruit and cinnamon. She wiped the sweat from her forehead with a dishtowel while she answered the door. Her dark hair hung in tight curls around her shoulders from the humidity of the kitchen. Tyler, her youngest at two years was fussing, perched on her left hip. When Christina saw it was the Garrets, she pulled open the door and motioned them to follow her back into the kitchen. The canner was only half full and three empty jars sat steaming on the counter waiting to be filled.

Skip had his hat in his hands, but he always did that when he came in the house and Christina didn't notice the long look on his face.

"Come on in and make yourselves at home. Zane's still in bed; he'll be sorry he missed you if he doesn't wake up soon." The boy worshiped his dad's partner and every picture he drew at school had a guy with a cowboy hat and a huge brown mustache.

Skip stood still as a statue, just inside the front door, as if he might need to make a quick escape. "Christina," he said, and she knew immediately something was wrong. Her name and the way he said it was enough to tell her—Skip had bad news. Though he was her age, Skip had become more like one of her own sons when Brenda left him. And like her sons, he wasn't hard for her to read. She handed Tyler to Kate and backed to the love seat where she swayed for a moment before sitting down. Skip started to speak but she held up her hand.

"Please, let me catch my breath a minute." Christina sat blinking and bit her lip. Fighting to keep an unseen weight from crushing her chest, she breathed deeply and tried to gain her composure. She nodded at Skip and opened her hands in her lap. "I think, I'm ready now for what you have to tell me."

Christina sat quietly and asked no questions while Skip explained to her how her best friend in the world was missing. She shook her head sadly when he mentioned the emergency locator signal and nodded when he described the Russian connection and the fugitive Leon Dahl.

"Russ Thompson has already told me I can go up as soon as we get a little more to go on. Chris, I'm worried too, but I still feel like everything will be okay." Skip sat beside Kate on the couch and scooted close to her for moral support.

"You know what's funny?" Christina said, looking back and forth at her two friends. "I'll bet I've had a hundred nightmares about him not coming home—from as far back as when he was in the army—but he always did. Now he's out there somewhere, probably hurt if he's even still alive and I'm sitting here fat, dumb, and happy with no idea anything was wrong." She shook her head. "It's strange. I always thought I'd know right away. I thought I'd feel it if he was in bad trouble."

"Maybe you would," Kate said, moving to the love seat and taking Christina's hand. "We have to keep up hope that everything is still all right."

Skip leaned forward, his elbows on his knees. "She's right. I trust Terry's judgement more than anyone else's in the world. If anything is wrong he's the one person who could make it come out all right."

Christina sighed sadly, half in a trance from the news. "Skip, tell me the truth. Knowing all that you know, what do you think happened? Do you really think he's okay?" Her pleading eyes scanned him to make certain he told her the truth.

"I believe he's still alive." Skip thought of Rockwell's visit. "As far as what's really going on, I can only guess. I imagine he and Paul have unwittingly gotten themselves in the middle of a Russian mob squabble."

Christina gave a halfhearted chuckle at the thought of her husband getting involved in anything unwittingly. "If he didn't have Paul with him, I'd accuse him of jumping into this on purpose."

Skip was sick with worry himself but used the opportunity to lighten the conversation. "I know what you mean. His compass always seems to point toward trouble. But don't you see? That's just what I'm talking about. He knows how to deal with stuff like this—he's used to it."

Christina rubbed her face with both hands, smoothing her hair back behind her head. "Have you talked to Tracy yet?"

"Not yet," Skip said softly. "I'm afraid she'll take it hard."

Christina let out a long breath. "She probably will. I think I should be the one to talk to her."

"Oh no," Kate said shaking her head. "You have enough to worry about already. We can do it."

"No, I can do more good. I'm afraid Tracy sees life as a black hole that's swallowing up everything she loves. I can do more good because we're in the same boat." Christina stood up. "Look I just need to be alone for a few minutes if it's all right."

Skip stood and touched her arm. "I see what you're saying, but are you sure you're up to it?"

She nodded and hugged Kate to finish the discussion on the matter.

"You need us to take the kids?" Kate asked.

"I'll get the neighbor to watch them when I go. In the meantime I'll let them sleep."

"I'm going to bring him home," Skip said when Christina hugged him. "You know I will."

"I know," she whispered in his ear. "I expect you to. But, remember not to do anything that will upset your beautiful wife. She worries about her husband too." She patted him softly on the back then stepped away so Kate could hear. "Now run along and leave me to myself for a while. I'll be all right."

Neither Skip nor Kate spoke as they walked out to their truck. Little Tyler banged on the living room window glass, waving good-bye through the curtains. Skip waved back, then opened Kate's door and told Belle to hop in the back seat. The dog had the habit of sitting in the front seat on the driver's side when Skip wasn't in the car so she could be nearer her man's smell. Shutting the passenger door he gave Tyler one last good-bye wave and walked around to the driver's side.

"You want to know what she whispered to me?" Skip was proud of his wife for not asking, but he knew she was curious and he didn't want anything to be left unsaid between them. He couldn't help but think he'd messed up somehow with Brenda, and whatever his mistake had been, he didn't want to duplicate it with Kate.

"If you can tell me. I don't want you to break a confidence."

"She's worried I'll run off and get hurt on you—or at the very least make you worry yourself sick over me."

"You're not, are you?"

"What? Get hurt?" Skip put the truck in gear.

"Yeah."

"Don't intend to."

"Okay then, there's no need for me to worry."

"Pioneer stock," Skip said under his breath.

"What does that mean?"

"Oh, I was just thinking about how lucky Terry and I are to be blessed with such stalwart women. You two are my heroes."

Kate laid her head against Skip's shoulder and sighed. She knew he was about to leave her for the love of a friend and it surprised her to find she expected him to do just that. "And you are mine," she said. "You are mine."

CHAPTER 16

Terry felt like someone had given him a boot to the ribs and left behind the boot. As a fighter, he was no stranger to pain and actually welcomed it most of the time. It reminded him he was alive and active in his training—growing and progressing. But this pain he felt now was a different sort of animal altogether. Now with his thoughts fuzzy, Terry found it hard to compartmentalize like he normally did. No matter how hard he tried to push the sickening ache from his ribs and right arm, it always worked its way back and threatened to shove him to his knees. He made it nearly five miles from the crash site before giving out altogether.

Terry was certain no one could see the discomfort in his eyes. He'd begun his training in the martial arts when he was three and had spent many hours working on his game face by the time he was baptized. His father taught him early on how much information the eyes could give away and Terry often used this knowledge to his advantage.

Ever dedicated to his training, when he was only thirteen Terry stepped on a roofing nail while he was running home from school. He'd been going fast and the nail ended up flush with the sole of his tennis shoe. His father was in the living room reading when he walked in the door and Terry realized this would be the perfect time to practice his self-control. Though the nail was relatively short, it stuck a good inch and a half into the ball of his foot and caused excruciating pain with every step. Slowing his walk, Terry stopped to talk with his father—his sensei— about the day. He learned that day about banishing his pain to another far-off part of his brain so he could deal with it in private. His father quizzed him about school and various things for a full five minutes and if he ever noticed any sign of pain in Terry's eyes, he didn't mention it. Then his mother came into the room with a saucer of cookies and immediately asked him what was wrong. That was the thing about mothers; strategy didn't always work with them the way it was supposed to.

But his mother was back in Montana, not lost with him in Alaska and he was sure none of the others saw the pain in his eyes. However, it was impossible to hide how wobbly he was on his feet. He knew Paul was worried. The boy hovered around him much of the time clearing away branches and helping him over the roughest spots in the trail. For a man who had always been a leader, it was humiliating. He hated to have anyone worry over him and wished he could send the boy away but the truth was, he needed his help.

Dahl paid close attention to Terry's condition. The prisoner's eyes still glowed yellow with fear of Petrov and he shuffled along like a crazed animal looking for any possibility of escape.

The spongy, uneven ground was hard on him and he moaned and grumbled to himself while he walked. It was hard on everyone. Though Terry felt they should put as much distance as they could between themselves and the downed airplane, he was grateful to move along slowly at Dahl's shuffling pace.

The terrain around the lake where they crashed was relatively flat and dry but less than a mile into their walk it turned into a spongy bog. Mountains lay ahead and there seemed no way around the series of lichen-covered rock hummocks and springy moss cut by dozens of rippling streams. Kit wanted to stay to the denser forest but in Terry's weakened condition she opted to take a more direct route and hop from pocket to pocket of the innumerable tiny forests of black spruce and birch doting the landscape. Some were as small as a quarter acre, some fifteen acres across.

Bugs proved to be more than a minor annoyance, especially for Kit and Terry who had to rely on repellent since Dahl and Paul had the only two head nets. The punkies seemed particularly interested in the wound on the back of Terry's bare head and swarmed around it in a tight black cloud the size of a fist, despite the thick layer of stinging white repellent. Whenever he or Paul tried to shoo them away, the swarm would scatter, then melt together again like quicksilver.

Kit had as many flying around her; they just weren't quite as concentrated in one particular spot. She waved her hands and arms in front of her as she led the way, keeping the bugs away from her nose and mouth as best she could. When the sun sank below the horizon, the insect attacks abated some but never completely disappeared.

Terry had heard stories of caribou stampeding to their deaths to escape tormenting flies and it was easy to see why. Very many hours of that kind of torment would drive a strong person insane, let alone one on the verge of shock.

Kit judged it to be about four in the morning when they stopped in a stand of spruce about the size of a football field. She hoped it would hide them if the Russians flew over again when the sun came up. Even at four in the morning it wasn't really what you could call dark—more like a foggy twilight that reminded Paul of the time of day when his mother would call him in from playing outside. That time of day when outside seemed light enough but once inside the bright house, the outside world seemed to grow dark immediately.

They chose a small clearing in the middle of a birch grove. The ground was high enough to be dry and years of falling birch leaves made it soft and springy. At Terry's direction Kit tied Dahl to the trunk of a tree as big around as her leg. She tested her knots a couple of times, making Dahl wince from the pulling. If she cared, it wasn't noticeable in her face. Once Kit felt assured the prisoner wouldn't get away, she let herself collapse on to the cool ground a few feet away with the others.

Looking at Kit, Terry knew she, like him would be asleep in minutes. There comes a point when stress and fatigue force the body to shut down no matter how hard you fight it. Dahl sat watching them, tied to his birch a few feet away.

"Leon," Terry said matter-of-factly, still hiding the pain in his eyes. "We're all going to sleep now. I'd advise you to do the same, but I want you to think about something before you do. If you did somehow get loose and get a chance to fire one of the guns, your Russian friends might hear it and come to investigate. Then they will kill you. If you get away tonight and I catch you, I will kill you."

Kit stretched in the shadows trying to make herself comfortable on the rocky ground. She wanted to show a united front with Terry. "If you consider your options, the only real bet is staying with us."

Dahl said nothing, but the way he slumped against his ropes told of his defeat. Terry leaned back on his good arm and watched the outlaw through the twilight haze while he finally let the waves of pure exhaustion wash over him. He had to try and make Dahl believe he could handle any problem, no matter how injured he looked. The outlaw needed to think escape was impossible, but gnawing at Terry's fevered brain as he tucked the pistol underneath him was the cold fact that once they all went to sleep, less than a half inch of nylon rope lay between the prisoner and freedom. If he tried to fight at that very instant, Terry wasn't sure who would win. He had to rely in large part on his bluff—but then, that's what strategy was all about.

If his experience against the Afghan rebels had taught Adrik Ivanovich anything, it was that a good escape plan is priceless. Many young commanders spent hours planning their attack down to the very letter but depended on luck to get them out if things didn't go well—if they bothered with it at all. Petrov was such a leader. He wanted to land at the first tiny speck of water they saw south of the crash site. While Adrik had enough faith in his abilities as a pilot to know he could get the plane down on such a lake, he also knew the limitations of his aircraft. Once down they would need a certain amount of space to take off.

Finally, after a good deal of patient argument, he was able to explain to his employer that they needed to find a larger lake quickly and leave enough fuel to get away. Once they got the information about the money from Dahl they wouldn't need him anymore, so they wouldn't have to worry about his added weight on the return trip. Adrik calculated just what he would need to land at one of the remote lodges on the chart. He knew they would have fuel there. What he did not have, Adrik knew he could steal from the enemy.

It was late in the evening by the time Adrik was able to find a lake that provided a suitable place to land, about ten miles due south of the crashed 180. There was still plenty of light and he was able to settle the plane onto the glassy water without a bump. The narrow dog-leg shaped lake had the added advantage of an inlet at the east end bordered on three sides by spruce and poplar. The small cove was just wide enough to park the plane. It would still be visible from above, but that could be taken care of with a little effort and some leafy branches.

Adrik's mind was already working on how to conceal the plane when he gunned the throttle enough to push them into the shaded hiding spot. The outstretched wings of the Cessna brushed the tops of a row of taller alder clumps along the shoreline and the morning air was instantly filled with a cloud of buzzing insects.

"The mosquitoes are going to be a problem," Adrik whispered to himself as he looked out the window at the cloud.

"Minor, compared to getting back to the lake and finding Dahl. You have put us much further away than I had hoped to be." Vasilii's hand was on the door handle. "Let us go quickly and get this thing done so we can get back to civilization."

"You should wait before you go outside," Adrik said, but his words were only halfhearted. He knew they would do no good.

"I already know about the insects," Vasilii sneered as he clicked open the door latch. "I am in a hurry Adrik, come ..." No sooner had the young Russian stepped out onto the bobbing pontoon than the slender alder branches and swamp grass erupted with hordes of mosquitoes and biting flies as if they had been waiting in ambush.

The swarm completely engulfed him. He spat and swore, clawing at his nose and eyes. For a moment, he forgot he was still on the water and had he not bumped into a wing strut he'd have run headlong into the lake in his panic. Still swatting and cursing he managed to crawl back into the plane, quickly slamming the door behind him against the attacking hordes.

Panting heavily, Petrov looked over at his pilot and shook his head in bitter contempt for Leon Dahl and all the trouble he had caused. "When I get my hands on that traitor, I may not kill him at all. Maybe I will strip him down and let the multitude of bloodsucking mosquitoes and flies do it." The young man shivered and smashed a mosquito in mid-meal across his forehead.

"Good idea," Adrik said, but he knew Vasilli would not be able to show that much restraint. Once Dahl told him what he wanted to know, it would all be over very quickly. He reached behind the seat and pulled a small green military-style canvas duffle, marked survival gear, into his lap. When he found what he was looking for he nodded smugly. "We will need these to make it more than ten feet from the airplane," he said, removing two olive green head nets and handing one to Petrov. The insects will still cause us much annoyance but we will survive." Adrik began to smear a thick white cream over his hands and the back of his neck. "The nets will protect our faces but we should put this on our hands."

The black cloud of mosquitoes hung suspended outside the plane, waiting as if they knew that the people inside would have to come out sooner or later. There were so many bugs that they blocked out much of the already diffused light and gave the place a surreal, buzzing haze. Some of the larger deer flies hovered just outside the door, periodically bouncing off the plexiglass windows. They knew there was fresh blood inside and would not leave without it.

"We should take the time to cut some branches and hide the aircraft," Adrik said, smiling inside at the torment on his pompous employer's face. He already knew about the insects. What a joke. Adrik considered himself a more than competent woodsman but if he knew anything it was that he didn't know everything. Insects couldn't be underestimated. Mosquitoes carried diseases that killed more people every year than all the other wild animals combined. And even if they didn't happen to carry any plagues, there were enough of the tiny creatures buzzing outside to drain a man dry in a matter of minutes—or cause them to kill themselves in madness.

Adrik looked across the small cockpit at Petrov and studied the man. He was talking about all the reasons why they should leave immediately and forget about hiding the plane. All the stupid reasons that Adrik knew would likely get them both killed or arrested. Petrov was such an imbecile he didn't realize how stupid he was. Many people were not smart enough to survive on their own in tough circumstances but some had enough good sense to know it. Not Vasilli. He would continue to think he was in charge, balking at every suggestion until it was laid out to him in minute detail. Adrik nodded subconsciously as the younger man talked. For now this behavior was laughable. The Petrovs paid him well and the possibility of his share of two million dollars and the chance to hunt the Indian woman made him willing to put up with a lot more nonsense than he usually would have, even from an employer. He eyed the .30 caliber rifle at his feet and sighed deeply. If Vasilii became too tiresome, his father would have to be informed of his unfortunate death at the hands of the wicked American, Dahl. There would be no reason for the old man not to believe him. He knew his son was weak—and he trusted Adrik.

There was no sport in killing Vasilii. Adrik had killed more people than he could count; some in war, some in business dealings. The only way it brought a thrill anymore was if the quarry was a challenge—like the Indian girl. She was smart and cunning. Adrik rolled his thick neck back and forth to rid himself of the tension Vasilii's whining gave him. Yes, she would be worth the chase and the kill.

In the end, Petrov grudgingly accepted the necessity of hiding the plane and agreed to spend time cutting alder branches to lay over the wings. Hungry mosquitoes dogged the men at every move with each leaf or twig they touched sending a dozen more into the air to harass them.

It was sweaty, uncomfortable work from inside the head nets and several times Petrov almost fell off the pontoons. After two hours, Adrik judged the wings covered enough to camouflage them from all but the most eagle-eyed pilot. Next, he turned his attention to the survival kit. The green canvass parachute bag contained a wealth of supplies—more than he wanted to carry. He didn't intend to signal anyone so he set aside things like signal flares and the first-aid kit. He'd been hurt before and come through it without fancy medical equipment to save him. If Vasilii got hurt ... well that was too bad for him. The big Russian made a pile of the things he thought would be of enough use to keep on the bank next to a clump of alders . Petrov eyed it suspiciously but said nothing, deferring at least for the moment to the more expert woodsman. There were extra shells for the .30 caliber carbine, matches, two feather sleeping bags, a small backpack, a fifty-foot piece of thin rope, and six prepackaged food bags that had the letters MRE printed on the side of their brown plastic envelopes.

Adrik recognized it as military food and smiled at the luck. The Russian military would never have provided such a feast.

He stuffed one of the sleeping bags inside the backpack along with three of the MREs. The others he stuffed into the roll of the remaining sleeping bag. Using a piece of cord, he made a loop around the bag and hung it over his shoulder. It was heavy enough to dig into the flesh of his shoulder but if Adrik noticed, he didn't seem to mind. The rifle had no sling so he held it in his right hand. Inside the survival duffle there was also a long hunting knife, but Adrik left it behind. He already had his own knife, with a handle of the finest European stag and a thick cleaving blade. It had been tried by fire, so to speak, and he preferred it to any other knife.

A hollow thumping, like the sound his wife made when she checked to see if a watermelon was ripe, brought Terry out of a tight, dreamless sleep. He'd hardly moved since closing his eyes and for the first few moments after hearing the sound thought he was bound or paralyzed. Slowly, his muscles began to cooperate and he was able to turn his head slightly in the direction of the thumping. He seemed to be looking at the world through a thin piece of gauze and had to struggle within himself to remember where he was. His memory and eyesight came floating back on the river of pain and nausea that flooded his body when he tried to rise up on his good arm. He turned as quickly as he could to see if Dahl had noticed and was relieved to see the outlaw was still asleep, sagging heavily against his ropes.

Off to Terry's right a grey camp robber pecked at the carcass of roasted beaver Kit brought from the crash, working to get at the bits of fat marbling the greasy meat. Each time the bird's black beak hit the dead animal, it made a dull thump.

Kit sat a few feet away surrounded by the cool mist of morning, watching the bird and slipping on her muddy boots. Her face and back of her hands were a garden of red welts and fly bites and her long black hair was covered with bits of grass and other debris from the forest floor.

"I hope I didn't wake you," she whispered so as not to disturb Paul, who lay curled between them in a foil space blanket like a giant baked potato.

"No." Terry's voice was hoarse. "You didn't wake me. It was

the jay eating our camp meat there." He looked slowly toward the beaver, a stiff neck not letting him do anything very fast.

"I know." She shook her head. "It was stupid of me to leave the meat in camp with us like that. We're lucky a bear didn't smell it and come in to give us trouble last night." She finished putting on her other boot and tiptoed over to Terry, stooping down with the water bottle. "I should have known better."

"Me too, but yesterday took a lot out of both of us." He took a long drink. Water was one thing they had plenty of and while it might contain quite a few microscopic critters there was nothing they could do about it at the moment. It usually took a few days for things like that to manifest themselves and Terry hoped they would be safely back in civilization by then. He gave Kit back the water bottle and looked at her poor, bitten face. "You'd better put some stuff on those bites so they don't get infected."

The corner of Kit's mouth was swollen from a bad mosquito bite but she smiled anyway and batted her long black eyelashes. "Why this is the way all us Indian princesses look in our natural state. A few bug bites won't hurt me. I'm too tough to get infected."

"That's what I used to think." Terry said, more pensive than glum.

""Well, what antibiotic we have is going to you and that's that. I need to get some kind of bandage on the back of your head before the punkies build a condo there." Kit rummaged through their meager supplies in the orange day pack and found the medical kit. She laid out tape, ointment and bandages, and looked at the back of Terry's head. The wound, counting the flesh the insects had carried away was now roughly the size of a dollar bill and ran from his right ear almost to the crown of his head. "We don't have any bandages big enough to cover this," she said looking at the first-aid supplies and thinking.

At length, she drew the long hunting knife from her belt.

"Just as I thought," Terry hung his head. "You're going to have to amputate."

"Yes I am." She wriggled out of her plaid over-shirt and laid it on her lap. "Part of this shirt is starting to bug me anyway and it should make you a nice bandage."

She worked at the tail of her shirt with the knife and ended up with a square the size of a bandanna. Knotting the corners, she fitted the makeshift hat over the back of Terry's head after dabbing on most of the antibiotic. The cloth was far from sterile. Kit had been wearing the shirt when they crashed and when she swam back out to the wreckage. She'd even slept in it but it was all they had and Kit hoped the ointment would keep any infection at bay for awhile at least. Terry hadn't flinched or said a word, though the process sent hot rivets of pain through the back of his eyes. A heavy bead of sweat formed across his brow, despite the chill of morning.

Kit sat back and looked at her nursing job. "Well you won't be winning any beauty contests but this should keep the buggies off that part of you anyway."

"Thank you." Terry smiled weakly. He was glad he didn't have to deal with Dahl for the moment and was sure he couldn't even have stood on his feet without assistance. "A man like me can't worry too much about how he looks. I suppose I've never been much of a slave to fashion."

"Listen," Kit said. "You need more rest before we move on. If you feel good enough to keep an eye on Dahl I'm going to go on a little scouting expedition toward the mountains and see if I can find us a place to hide out. There are a few old trapper cabins in these hills. Maybe I can stumble on to one. That would at least give us a fighting chance if the Russians find us."

Terry didn't like the idea of Kit going off alone but she was right, he did need more rest. She was capable enough. After all, if it weren't for her Terry knew he would likely still be at the bottom of the lake, stuck in the plane.

"Be careful," he finally said. "And watch your trail. We don't know how good these Russians are in he woods. They could be trackers, so you best be careful where you put your feet."

Kit nodded. "I will. Do you want me to wake Paul up before I go or do you want me to let him bake a little longer?"

"Let him sleep. I'll be all right, you just watch yourself out there."

Kit picked up the beaver carcass and carved off a back haunch. It was a big animal and the meat was rich so the chunk was enough for three people. "Here's breakfast. I'll take the rest and cache it down in the permafrost out of camp a ways. If a bear doesn't get it before I come back, we'll have the rest for supper."

Terry couldn't help but smile as he watched the young Athabascan woman walk gingerly through the trees with the rest of the beaver in one hand and the rifle in the other, a large square of cloth missing from the back of her plaid shirt. The girl had probably never had a day's training in her life but she already walked with the confident, floating stride of a martial artist. He and Paul were fortunate to come under the care of this stout little Native woman, very fortunate indeed.

Had it not been for Port's recent visit, Terry might have thought he was seeing things.

"Reduced to eatin' flat-tailed rat, I see," Rockwell said, hunkering down next to his friend. "It's better than the alternative I reckon."

"That it is, Port. That it is." Terry leaned back against a black spruce. "I don't suppose you could get a message to Skip and tell him to come pick us up?"

The old gunman shook his head sadly. " Fraid I can't tell him exactly where you are. Wish I could but it don't work that way. I did tell him to get a move-on, though, and he already has a fair idea about where to start looking. How are you feeling anyway?"

"Been better but I guess I'll live." Terry raised his eyebrows and looked at Port. It suddenly dawned on him that he might not. "You're not looking for a sidekick in the great beyond are you?"

" Well, no." The old man shrugged. " I don't think so, at least. Anyway, they don't tell me about that stuff."

Terry sighed and closed his eyes. "I guess that's a relief. You know, I don't care much for this mortal feeling. I know I'm just a man but it's hard for me to depend on someone else to help me. I hardly ever even catch a cold. I remember one time I got the flu pretty bad. I wanted to go to work but my wife wouldn't let me. She said some weaker soul might catch it. Said she figured if a germ was bad enough to make me sick, it would kill anyone else."

"I know what you mean," Port nodded, scratching his jaw. "I think when you carry a gun and a badge for a livin' you get in the habit of feelin' all godlike—like we ride down from Mount Olympus to deal with the problems of mere mortals only every once in a while."

"That's about right. I forget sometimes that I can actually get hurt." Terry lightly touched the back of his head. "And hurt bad, at that."

"Tell me about it," Port said. "I cut my locks off to make a wig for a friend once. She lost her hair to the fever. I mean to tell you,

I never felt so vulnerable in all my life. I know what you mean, it's a rotten feeling." Rockwell took a deep breath, remembering, then studied Paul, wrapped in his foil blanket. "So how's the young spud taking all this?"

"I don't know. With all that's gone on in the past year, I wonder if this isn't all too much for him." Terry forgot about his own aches for a moment and looked over at the boy. "He was pretty quiet yesterday. He's already full of anger, I worry about all this piling on top of him. He was already on the verge of exploding when we came on this trip."

Rockwell drew lines in the dirt with a broken birch twig. "I don't reckon I ever told you about my minin' days did I?"

"No."

"Well, I wasn't really a miner. I handled the mules for some folks that were looking for some rock or another down around Moab in southern Utah. Anyhow, in all the digging, those miners struck some sort of swamp gas they hadn't counted on and it caught fire."

Rockwell's grey eyes glistened while he relived the sight of the blaze. "Well sir, the fire was a bad one, I'm here to tell you. Shot up like a huge orange mare's tail, forty or fifty feet into the air. Those buzzards tried everything they could think of to put out that fire. Water didn't work and no one could get close enough to get a cap on it. Well, there was this rangy whelp of a cuss helping me with the mules who was fresh off the boat from Europe, I can't recollect where exactly. Lars, I think his name was. Anyhow, he'd had some experience with swamp gas. He came up with the idea of draggin' a load of dynamite into the fire on a chain to blow out the whole shebang like a big birthday candle." Port pointed the stick at Terry. "And you know what? It worked. Seems it took one heck of a big bang to knock out a fire like that one."

Terry nodded thoughtfully but didn't speak.

"So," the old gunfighter winked a knowing eye. "You get what I'm sayin'." He looked over his shoulder at Dahl. "Your prisoner is startin' to stir, so I'd best get gone. You watch yourself, Brother McGreggor."

Before Terry could reply Rockwell stepped into the trees and was gone.

Kit buried the rest of the beaver in a layer of permafrost about half a mile out of camp. She used the hunting knife to cut a layer of spongy sod. Lifting it out carefully, she chopped at the milky green sheet of ice underneath. When she had a small trough big enough for the meat, she laid the piece of sod back over the top and patted down the edges so a human observer wouldn't be able to find her hiding spot. Of course anything with a nose that happened on the spot would dig up the meat in no time, no matter how well she concealed her tracks, but there was nothing she could do about that. Remembering the time she lost a bunch of fish she cached while fishing with her mother, she placed three willow twigs in strategic, camouflaged locations to mark her hiding spot and checked around her to get her bearings. After all, her mother was right when she'd pointed out there was no use hiding game if you couldn't find it again.

That small chore done, Kit set off through the sparse woods toward the distant mountains. There was no real trail and she meandered slightly this way and that, trying to keep to dry ground. She trotted when the footing permitted, as much to get away from the bugs as to gain time. She had her own private cloud, dark enough to see from a quarter mile away, that harried and harassed her every at step.

The land rolled deceptively and though she was often out of the thick trees, Kit didn't get a glimpse of the mountains she aimed for until an hour past the beaver cache. A large, mostly open valley still separated her from the nearest green foothills she hoped would offer some relief from the bugs and sloppy muskeg. Her wool pants were soaked above the knees and stained tea-colored from constantly breaking though the muck into the water below. Every step through the vegetation brought to life more mosquitoes and biting flies.

From her slightly higher vantage point the valley below looked like a broken, brown mirror with thousands of small streams shattered across its floor. A thin coat of snow—termination dust marking the end of summer—coated the tops of the higher hills. It was still too warm for the snow to stick so it melted and ran into the valley, raising the level of the river snaking its way across the flat toward the forest. She could tell from a distance that the river was too high to cross, especially for Terry. But standing on the small ridge, Kit knew that it didn't matter how wide or swift the river was, Terry was in no shape to make it this far across such a bug-infested swamp. She felt stupid for thinking she could find a place for them to hide, but kept scanning the valley out of habit. Her mother often said that most people didn't see their way because they didn't take the time to look.

Kit wiped her eyes with the cuff of her shirt and looked hard at the valley floor to her right. The dark line of spruces cut a long crescent from the bottom of the ridge she stood on to the base of the mountains. It was odd to see such a precise line except on a river bank and Kit realized they were bordered by a long embankment of gravel. A moraine, left there from a glacier ages before. The find made her heart beat faster and she turned to see that the gravel line ran behind her not a half a mile away from where the others waited in the trees. McGreggor could make it half a mile even in the unforgiving forest. Once he made it to the moraine, he'd have a perfect highway.

Excited by her find, Kit waved her hand in front her face to keep the bugs out of her nose and started at a fast trot down the ridge. She was at the river in no time and was happy to find that though the moraine had been somewhat washed away by seasonal flooding, the gravel bed went deep into the earth and the water was less than a foot deep where it flowed as much through the rock highway as over it.

Of course, everything that knew about the moraine used it as a trail and countless tracks dotted the area around the river. Kit recognized moose and wolf near the water's edge and further up, as the mud turned into dry gravel again, she saw the huge tracks of a grizzly. No matter how long she lived in the bush, the great animal always made her hair stand on end. There was really no way to tell how large a bear was just from the size of its tracks. Some bears have big feet and little bodies and others have little stubby feet compared to their gargantuan size. These tracks were big and deep and the depth told Kit it was a bear of respectable stature. Stooping low, she put the elbow of her left arm in the heel track of the grizzly and laid her forearm out to measure. She sucked in a quick breath when she realized the claws on the track hit her in the middle of her palm.

It was big enough to be from an old boar. They were usually pretty crotchety and no fun at all to butt heads with. The track looked to be old, though, so she kept her trail and trotted on toward the mountain.

After leaving the moraine, she'd tried to keep to the lower, more easily traveled mountains. Her instinct told her to go up to get away from trouble but she supposed that was the pilot in her. She surprised several spruce hens along the way and made mental notes of all the game trails she ran across. Tiny bits of information like this became all-important in a survival situation.

A little more than a mile into the foothills, Kit turned up a small valley. The landscape was literally wrinkled with such furrows and she could have gone up any one of them. Since she had no real destination in mind, she followed her nose, acting on instinct. As it happened, her instinct paid off. The underbrush thinned the higher she went up the valley, as if rain had washed most of the seeds down to pile up at the base of the hills. Small groups of twisted spruce scattered across the mountain face and low-bush blueberry shrubs carpeted the lower slopes. Here and there a rivulet tumbled down among the scattered rocks and fed a larger stream eventually flowing into the Ladue River.

About halfway up the little canyon another even smaller trench shot off to Kit's right. Still following her gut, the sturdy little Indian girl scrambled up a small rick slide to the almost hidden valley. Not more than a hundred feet across at it's widest point, it seemed not much more than a big ditch. A tiny stream raced swift and clear through pockets of golden leafed birch only to disappear in the pile of rock and gravel that all but obscured the valley's entrance.

"Water … protection from the wind … plenty of firewood …" Kit whispered, breathing faster from the excitement of having stumbled onto such a lovely spot. "A perfect place for …" Her eyes scanned the slopes until they stopped on a loose fan of light grey scree about thirty feet up, "a mine."

Kit knew this particular area of the Yukon was famous for its lost gold mines. Most were lost for good reason—they didn't have any gold—but she didn't care about gold, she needed shelter. No matter what kind of mine this was, lost or just plain abandoned, it would offer that. It was a decent climb along the side hill to get to the entrance and she was exhausted. The sun was already starting its long downward arc toward the horizon. Kit still had to get all the way back to the others and make a return trip. Standing to rest a few more moments, she looked up at the mine and smiled at her good fortune. If she could only get Terry this far he might have a chance—if the Russians hadn't gotten to them or Leon hadn't escaped and killed everyone while she was gone. Too many ifs, she thought to herself and turned back down the valley toward the moraine. Every second she was away from Terry and the others added a layer of worry to Kit's mind. Time was crucial now. Terry's strength was failing fast and she had to get him to the shelter before he was too sick to move. Then she could worry about getting them out.

As pilot, Kit felt a keen sense of responsibility to her passengers and that sense followed her to the ground. Terry's health worried her more than even the Russians. He was a good man, but her father had proved that good men died whether you wanted them to or not. As much as she wanted McGreggor to pull through for his own sake, she wanted it for Paul. His eyes were dark already even on the rare occasions when she'd seen him smile. Kit knew what the death of her own father had done to her and she'd been an adult. As arbitrary as life was, losing a father as well as a father figure in a year's time seemed too unfair and Kit made a silent pledge to herself to keep that from happening.

CHAPTER 17

Saturday

It always amazed Skip how an airline could assign seats to someone without checking to see how tall they were. The flight from Missoula to Edmonton was bearable because he had gotten a bulkhead seat, but this commuter sardine can that was taking him to Dawson City, Yukon, was not meant to hold someone as tall as Skip Garret. The fact he had to give up his gun to fly into Canada had already put him in a bad mood, and the cramped conditions and drone of the tiny prop-driven plane just added to his frustration. The pilot didn't seem to be paying near enough attention in his opinion.

The whole thought of leaving mother earth where there were plenty of good horses seemed to him to be a crime against nature. He'd made it through his teenage years without ever getting near an airplane and had hoped against hope he'd get a mission call to a state he could get to by bus. When he got his call to Japan, his streak ended. The eleven-hour flight was so torturous to his mind and body he extended his mission for two months just to put off another flight, even if it was back home.

There was a tight, stuffy atmosphere in the commuter plane and a peculiar, stale odor that made it hard for Skip to take a deep breath. Flying, worrying about Terry and Paul, going unarmed, and leaving Kate behind tore at Skip's gut. He fiddled with the spigot above his seat and put the air on full force. Even the cool wind in his face was not enough the blow his bad feelings away.

The Dramamine he'd taken in Edmonton kept his stomach at a slow churn. He was queasy enough to keep his surly mood but calm enough to think a little about the mission at hand.

Unlike every movie supervisor stereotype, Russ Thompson had gone above and beyond his duty to grease the skids for Skip to work with the Canadians on their search. The Emergency Locator transmission had narrowed the location down some and most of the search efforts were being launched from a ranch outside Dawson City toward the Alaska border. Thompson's contacts put him in touch with a Royal Canadian Mounted Police Constable named Mackenzie Roberson who was stationed in Dawson City and knew the area. He apparently had a special interest in the bush pilot who'd been flying Terry and Paul. As far as Skip could tell they were practically engaged. He hadn't seemed to mind that some American lawman was flying up to horn in on the search and Skip wondered how he might have felt in a similar situation.

Since Missoula was not too far from the Canadian border, Skip had worked with the RCMP on several occasions and always found them top-notch lawmen. He'd checked out this Roberson fellow and found out he'd been three years on the RCMP Musical Ride mounted drill team. Skip had seen them perform at the Calgary Stampede and was supremely impressed. If he couldn't carry a gun in Canada at least he'd be able to ride with another person who knew horses. He took an envelope from his vest pocket and looked at the scribbling on the back. He was supposed to meet someone named Murphy at the airport in Dawson City who would take him to a ranch outside town where he could hook up with Roberson. Reading on the plane made his stomach churn even more so he put the envelope away and leaned his head back against the seat, letting his hat slide forward to shade his eyes. Even without his trusty forty-five it would be nice to get out of this rolling airplane and onto a good steady horse.

The only good thing about the sardine can was that it didn't carry many people so Skip was able to get his bags right away. An attendant wearing a green Tuffy jacket wheeled out a dolly with a tan pet carrier. Skip squatted down next to the cage and Belle greeted him with a high pitched-yap. Flying didn't seem to bother her as much as being cooped up in the carrier. He paid the attendant to store the carrier for him at the airport and let the dog out. As usual, she stayed at her man's heels, looking up at him for direction at every turn. Skip hadn't mentioned to Russ that he was bringing the dog but he hardly ever traveled without her. Terry had been surprised when Skip asked him to keep her while he and Kate went on their honeymoon. Besides the fact that he just plain wanted her along, Skip reasoned that she was familiar with Terry and Paul both and could help with the tracking if the need arose.

"Cute dog," a voice said from behind while Skip was busy scratching Belle behind the ears. He turned to see a freckle-nosed blond woman wearing a blue Alaska State Troopers uniform.

Skip offered a hand and studied her badge. " Skip Garret. I must have taken a wrong turn back there some where. I'm supposed to be in Canada."

"Jill Murphy, out of Tok, Alaska. No wrong turns, you're in the right place. We blueshirts help the redshirts across the border every chance we get." Skip noticed that she wore a spit-shined Sam Browne belt but no holster or sidearm. "I'm detailed over here to help coordinate the search in case it leads to U.S. soil. Russ Thompson from your office called and told us to be expecting you."

"Good old Russ. He's always taking care of me," he said as much to himself as to the young trooper. In a world where supervisors seemed to be the front line officer's mortal enemy, Russ Thompson had turned out to be a gem.

Murphy bent down and gave Belle a rub on the back. "He told me to look for a tall cowboy with an oversized mustache and a blue dog following him around. He said he was pretending he didn't know you brought the dog. Seems like a nice boss."

Skip chuckled. Yeah, Russ was a gem all right.

"If you've got your stuff, I guess we should get out there and get back to the search." She stood. "It's a bit of a drive, eh."

Skip smiled, seeing that even an Alaskan living close enough to Canada wasn't immune to picking up the lilting *eh* peculiar to Canadian speech. "A drive in the car suits me right down to the bones. I'll go about any way you want as long as I don't have to fly. I need to get my land legs back."

Trooper Murphy gave him a puzzled laugh and walked to her state-issued Chevy Tahoe. The drive out of Dawson on Highway Nine look a little over an hour. Skip was impressed by the wildness of the terrain and compared it to what Montana must have been like a hundred years before he ever got there. The pretty trooper acted as a tour guide and pointed out interesting tidbits of information about fishing in the streams they crossed; telling the tale of a roadside cafe owner who'd shot a grizzly bear coming in her open kitchen window to steal a rhubarb pie the week before.

Steering the car with her knees, the pretty young trooper took a flat red box out of her vest pocket. Giving the box a hard smack on the steering wheel, she opened it and unwrapped the broken pieces of hard caramel candy inside. "Want some Macintosh toffee? It's good stuff, eh. I've never been able to find it in the States."

Skip looked at the candy and shook his head. "No thanks. It would likely pull my fillings out."

Trooper Murphy got herself a piece and replaced the box in her pocket. Skip looked out the window. Some stretches of the road were dry and dust-choked while others, where mountains shaded or streams crossed, were lush and green. The land had a quality to it that reminded Skip of what a person would get if they took the ingredients for Texas and Montana and shook them up in a bottle.

The Silvertip Ranch acted as base station for operations during the search and Skip was happy to see a stable full of fat mountain horses saddled and munching on hay when Trooper Murphy wheeled her Chevy into the drive. A pack string of six draft mules stood loaded and tied to the corral fence. Skip could see from some distance away that the animals had been packed by someone who knew his stuff and after thanking the trooper for the ride he grabbed his duffle and headed off with Belle to investigate.

The community of true-to-the-bone packers was a small one. The experts had certain quirks and idiosyncracies that set their work off from run-of-the-mill school-trained packers and made them recognizable to the trained eye. You couldn't always tell exactly which expert had loaded an animal, but you could sure enough tell it was done by someone who had more training than a ten-day school from an ad in the back of a magazine. These mules were loaded with Deckers, the hooped pack saddles preferred by people who wanted to move heavy, odd-sized loads. The whole shebang was tied on with a rope on either side that ran around each load in a series of knots that had names like *crow's foot* and *barrel hitch*. A good packer tied his load so it was balanced and easy on the horse. An expert packer tied his load so he could untie it with one quick jerk in the right spot, making it easy on the horse and himself.

Skip leaned against the top rail of the corral and studied the loaded mules. If he was going to find Terry and Paul, whoever had packed these mules was the kind of person he could do it with. He heard footsteps and looked down at Belle. "I used to know a fellow that did a fair job at loading packsaddles. I expect whoever did these learned from him."

"Skiparoo Garret," came the booming voice from behind him. "Is that you?"

Skip turned to see a short, redheaded man with a barrel chest and a drooping Yosemite Sam mustache. "Well, Bull Witherspoon." He stuck out his hand while Belle gave the man a hello bark.

"Enough of this handshaking horse hockey," Witherspoon said, pulling Skip to him in a crushing bear hug. "How long has it been boy? Five, six years?"

"More like eight," Skip said, straightening his hat. "A long time."

When Skip was in college he earned extra money shoeing horses. Bull, a hunting guide in Montana at the time, had a summer home in Utah and kept several of his horses there. The man was a competent farrier himself but a young mule had gone over backward with him the previous year and injured his back. The accident hadn't stopped him from riding but it did create the need for a temporary shoer. As a returned missionary and newly married man going to college, Skip needed all the work he could get.

"How's that wife of yours?" Bull let go a roaring laugh. "I remember she used to get so mad at me for keeping you over at my place talking about horses till late into the evening. It wasn't my fault you needed a real education to go along with that stuff they were teaching you in college."

Skip propped a boot on the bottom rail of the fence. "She moved out a couple of years ago. Things never did get much better after we moved back to Texas. But don't think I'm not happy. I'm married to a wonderful woman named Kate and we have a youngster on the way."

"Well that's good." Witherspoon slapped him on the back. "I always saw you as the family-raisin' sort of man. What did you do with my little horse? Did Brenda Jo get to keep her?"

"No," Skip grinned sheepishly. "I still have her. You told me it was a stupid idea to name her after my wife, but it seemed like a good idea at the time."

"I never said it was stupid. I said it was like getting a tattoo of your girlfriend's name on your forehead. I guess I just had a feeling about you and that particular woman." Witherspoon chewed on the long end of his mustache. "Tell me, what does your new wife think about having a horse named B.J.?"

"I dropped B.J. and just call her the dun mare now. It makes things a lot simpler."

"So you got any horses named Kate yet?"

Skip chuckled at the thought. "No, but it wouldn't matter this time. This one's in it for the long haul."

Bull took a long look at his old friend. "You're getting older, boy. I guess I must be getting ancient. So if you got a wife that's ready to foal and you're all the way up in the Yukon, you must be up here for the search. I heard one of the guys missing is a U.S. Marshal."

The talk of Terry brought Skip back to the reality of the moment after his happy reunion. "He's my partner. I'm supposed to meet a Constable Mackenzie Roberson with the R.C.M.P. and join up with him for the search. You know where he is?"

"I do, but I can't picture you doing much searchin' with him." Witherspoon shrugged and nodded toward a long wooden barn. "Follow me, he's right on the other side here."

"There must be some mistake," Skip stammered when they reached the other side of the barn.

"No sir, that's Mac Roberson all right. I oughta know, too, cause he threw me in jail not more than a month ago for a little misunderstandin' in a bar if you know what I mean. That's him right beside his plane there."

Skip put a hand on his friend's shoulder. "But the horses out front? Aren't we going to use them on the search?"

"Not hardly. Nobody even knows where to look yet. Smartest bet is by plane so far. Besides those are my ponies, all saddled up for a load of Japanese tourists wanting five days of cowboy life in the Canadian wilderness." Bull noticed the sallow look of his young friends face. "You okay, Skiparoo? You look like you just swallowed a shoeing nail."

"I can't believe I have to get in another plane."

"That's right, you don't care much for flyin'. Don't worry though, Mac's one of the best. Him and his girlfriend Kit are two of the finest bush pilots in the north."

The roar of a bus filled with Bull's Japanese guests interrupted them as it pulled off the road and stopped in front of the barn. "Sorry, but I got to go, Skip." Witherspoon gathered up his friend for another quick handshake. "I've got to get these folks introduced to their horses. I wish you were along to help me talk to these folks. We'll get together again before you head south, though. You'll be all right with Mac. Just be patient with him, he's kinda quiet."

Constable Mackenzie Roberson was securing the engine cowling on his red-and-white Piper Super Cub when Skip walked up behind him. The Mountie cleaned his right hand on a red shop rag before extending it for a firm handshake. "You must be Deputy Garret, eh?"

"That I am sir," Skip said, shaking the hand and eyeing the man it was attached to.

Roberson was dressed in the work uniform of an RCMP—dark blue pants and brown knee boots that came up as high as Skip's riding boots, but had a flat walking heel. The red serge tunic of the old-time mounted police had been replaced by a long-sleeved, light blue shirt. On top of that Roberson sported a fuzzy, tan fleece jacket with the Mountie's buffalo head crest and their motto—*Maintiens le Droit* embroidered in gold. Maintain the Right. His brown duty belt was polished to match his boots and a flap holster covered the butt of a stainless steel revolver.

Skip let go of Roberson's hand. The man didn't wear a hat but at least he shot a revolver. His dark hair was cropped above his ears and although he was still in his late twenties, sported a one inch shock of grey over his right temple.

"I was sort of led to believe we'd be horseback with all your Musical Ride background," Skip said, giving the Super Cub a doleful look.

Roberson's lips curled up into just the slightest smile. "I wouldn't mind riding myself, but we can cover more ground in the bird. They told me you didn't care much for flying."

"Don't care much for tetanus shots either," Skip said, unwilling to talk about his weakness with someone he'd just met. "But I get them when I need to."

"I know what you mean." Roberson nodded in genuine understanding. "When it's your friend out there you're willing to do just about anything, eh. I'm close to the missing pilot myself."

Skip scuffed at the ground not knowing what to say. The only thing showing any worry at all on this guy was a twitch in his right eye. Other than that he could have been going up on a Saturday afternoon flightseeing trip.

"Handsome dog," the Mountie gestured with the shop rag at Belle. He didn't want to think about Kit out there and hurt any more than Skip wanted to think about Terry or Paul. "Mind if I pet her?"

"That's up to her, I guess." Skip's voice had an edge to it. He knew his cruddy attitude was caused in great part by his sour stomach. Still, he couldn't help but feel a little animosity toward a person whose aim was to take him up in a plane no bigger than the kites he used to play with as a kid. It wasn't even made out of metal, for crying out loud. To make matters worse Belle was fawning all over the guy and soaked up his attention like a dry sponge.

"You're a pretty lass eh," the young constable said, scratching the dog's neck with both hands. "Yes, you are a pretty lass."

Roberson had a reputation as a hard lawman but there was a bit of a naive look in his eye. Skip realized his attitude was slipping, and it was no fault of Roberson's. He just couldn't warm up to the guy. He'd had a missionary companion or two like that in Japan. To top it all off, Belle who was one to mistrust strangers—particularly people Skip didn't like—had already rolled over and lay with her tongue lolling, getting a good belly rub she usually reserved for Skip.

Roberson looked up. "I don't know how she'd do in the Cub. Some dogs tend to get pretty ill, eh."

"No. I don't want to put her through that. I only brought her because I thought we'd be on horses. She's smart enough to take care of herself here for a while if I leave her behind." Skip lived the kind of lifestyle where a cow dog was rarely a liability and he was used to taking her everywhere he went. The back seat of this little plane seemed out of the question. He didn't want to get in the thing himself, so he sure wasn't going to ask his favorite dog to do it. "You come back here to fuel up right?"

"Correct," Roberson said. "The ranch serves as base

camp. We'll take our meals here when it's too dark to search any longer."

"Okay then, give me a chance to stow my gear and settle the dog. I won't be five minutes." Skip was surprised at how eager he sounded to get into what he considered nothing more than a winged coffin.

"Carry on then," Roberson looked back at his airplane. "I still have to give the Cub another quick preflight before we take her back up. Ten minutes should be about right."

The seat of the commuter plane was spacious as a sofa compared to the back seat of the Super Cub. It was a padded metal hinged affair that reminded Skip more of some ancient instrument of torture than a place to sit. The angle put his knees and elbows into constant competition for space.

Roberson handed a set of green headphones over his shoulder. "You should wear these. It gets a bit loud in here, eh." He looked back so see that Skip put them on correctly. "And if you get sick to your stomach, make sure and move the mike out of the way."

Skip adjusted the headset and blew into the mouthpiece to see if it was working. The second motion sickness pill of the day had dried his mouth and added a degree or two to his already grumpy attitude.

Roberson yelled, "Clear!" out his open window before pulling it shut, then started the engine. After one loud roar and a puff of grey smoke that seemed to Skip to be a bit on the unhealthy side, the little plane bounced down the gravel runway, then turned into the wind for takeoff.

"Search control," the Mountie said, pushing a button on his control stick and startling Skip with the sudden noise in his ears. "This is Piper Charlie-One-Seven-Sierra-Papa going up for another look. Over."

Skip heard a spray of static, then a soft female voice. "Roger, Seven-Sierra-Papa. Hello Mac," the voice said. It didn't sound to Skip like the girl behind it was much over fourteen. "Grid Echo-Zero-Seven has yet to be searched if you want to try over there, eh."

"Roger that, "Roberson said. "Where's your dad flying now?"

"Over by the Victoria Burn area." There was a rattle of paper over the open mike. "That's Bravo-One-One on the grid map."

"Roger. We'll stay in touch then. By the way Carol, I've got the visiting marshal from the States on board with me."

"I'll make a note," Carol said. "And good hunting Mac."

"Thanks. Good day then." Roberson increased the power and released the brakes. "That was Carol Demming. Her dad's likely the best pilot in the Yukon. It might help to know that we've got some very capable pilots in the air searching."

Skip nodded but didn't speak. He was grateful for all the local interest but at that very moment he wanted Roberson to think about flying the flimsy airplane, not engage him in a long conversation.

Even with two big men aboard, the Super Cub literally bounded from the runway with only a short takeoff roll. Skip closed his eyes, feeling like he'd left his stomach back on the gravel strip. He was suddenly very grateful he'd taken the second pill, dry mouth or not. Roberson banked the plane sharply to the west, gaining altitude in the turn. Since Skip sat directly behind the pilot and the wings of the Cub were mounted on top, he had an unobstructed view from both sides of the plane of his beloved earth as they left it behind.

To make matters worse, when Roberson took the Cub over the edge of the ranch near the corrals, Skip was able to see Bull Witherspoon on his massive black-and-white paint horse leading a string of pack mules and a broken line of Japanese tourists. Belle scampered through the birch trees after the mounted caravan, yapping wildly and having the time of her life.

Skip pressed his face against the cool plexiglass window to get as long a look as possible while the plane overflew the procession. That was how a man was meant to travel. When the horses were behind him and out of sight, he leaned back in the cramped folding seat and resigned himself to a day of queasy worry.

CHAPTER 18

About the time Skip wedged himself into the airplane heading from Missoula to the Yukon Territory, Kit prepared to lead her little group back to the relative shelter and safety of the mine. Her return trip the previous day had taken every ounce of her strength even with the added ease of traveling on the moraine.

On the way back she'd taken time to check her cache. As she had feared, the meat was gone. Tiny tracks showed where a fox made off with it. So the group made do with a supper of cool water. Paul picked a few handfuls of blueberries growing near camp but there weren't enough to make a meal and their tart sweetness only served to remind them of how hungry they really were. Dahl worried about the Russians; the thought of a cook fire gave him the shakes and he was just as happy to go without food. Somehow, even the thought of starving to death was more appealing than what Vasilii Petrov would surely have planned for him.

With their meager supplies, it didn't take long to pack. Two nights in the same spot left ample evidence that someone had been there. There were too many tracks to hide completely, particularly since Terry had to use Paul's walking stick to get around. Dahl alone had kicked up so much of the fragile topsoil around his tree, it was impossible to disguise the fact someone had been tied there.

After a bit of thinking, Terry decided not to even try. The best idea was to quickly leave an easily trackable false trail out of camp in the opposite direction. At best it would get them lost, at worst maybe it would slow them down and give rescuers a little more time. Kit told him the moraine was off to the northeast, so he planned his counter-tracking trail to go west, heading deeper into the spruce forest.

Using the opportunity to teach Paul a little about tracking, Terry pointed out what a good tracker looked for when he hunts for sign. Of course, one of those things is footprints. They often tell much of the story, but some types of terrain don't leave very clear prints. When tracks are visible, the stride length can be measured and when the tracks disappear the tracker can make an educated guess about where the next track should be. If the person being tracked jumped or changed his stride, the tracker might be confused, but those kind of actions left telltale marks and someone with experience knew how to read them.

Terry wished he could leave the false trail himself but with his head throbbing and the world spinning around him with every step, he had a hard time walking a straight line. Giving Paul his walking stick, Terry directed him to use it like he had a sprained ankle and walk out of camp a few hundred yards with Kit until they got to some dry ground that didn't leave tracks. As best they could, he wanted them to retrace their tracks so all their footprints would be in the same direction. Paul seemed to enjoy the trickery and Kit, though eager to get on the move, understood the importance of keeping the Russians off their trail.

Dahl shook his head in disgust. He opened his mouth to speak but a look from Terry caused him to close it again.

Once the false trail was completed, Kit led the group toward the moraine. Dahl followed behind her, watching his step as best he could in the hobbles. Terry carried the walking stick but leaned on Paul for support to minimize his impact on the trail.

What the forest in between their camp and the moraine lacked in bogs and biting insects, it more than made up for in thick underbrush and devil's club that clawed at the arms and faces of the little group. When the sharp, hairlike thorns attacked a leg or arm, they broke off under the skin and irritated them more than even mosquitoes. Several times, birch limbs and alder branches whipped back on the outlaw. With his hands tied to his waist he was unable to fend them off. "I'm being shredded alive here," he whined. No one else said a word.

Paul chuckled when Dahl stumbled and lost his balance completely in a particularly gruesome bramble of thorny devil's club, causing him to yowl in pain.

Terry tapped the boy on his shoulder and shook his head slightly. "Don't take comfort in his pain." He spoke haltingly, in between ragged breaths.

"But it's his fault we're here at all." Paul kept walking beside Terry but didn't look up. The bill of his cap was pulled low to hide his eyes. "You said yourself you'd kill him."

"And I will if he makes me," Terry sighed, dizzier from the effort of speaking. "But I hope for your sake I don't have to, Paul."

The boy stared at the ground as he walked. "If I had a gun I'd go ahead and do it. You can't change people like him."

Terry patted his young friend on the shoulder. His own words seemed doubly loud in his ears as if he were shouting. The throbbing whoosh in the back of his head made carrying on any sort of conversation almost intolerable. He avoided talking as much as he could, afraid he might sound incoherent and tip Dahl off to how bad his condition really was. Talking wasn't going to change the way Paul felt anyway.

Once they reached the moraine the group made surprisingly good time. The trees off to the left of the gravel ridge offered protection in the event the Russians flew over again and the bare rocky highway made them highly visible if friendly aircraft happened to be in the area. But it didn't matter. Nothing, not even a raven, flew over them all day long.

At the river crossing, Paul found tracks left by the giant grizzly and whistled under his breath marveling at their size. "I wish I had a camera. No one would believe a bear this big." He pointed to his feet which were both standing inside the huge track with plenty of room to spare.

"I'd believe you. I've seen some awfully big bear. Let's just hope we don't meet this one." Kit gave Paul a handful of soft orange fruit. "Rose hips. Give these to Terry, then help me pick more before we go." She pinched one of the fragile buds between her fingers. "There's gobs of vitamin C in each of these little guys. Be careful to eat only the jelly though. These hairy little seeds tickle the gizzard too much and might upset your stomach."

"Roger that," Paul said, copying Kit's pilot voice before trotting off to give the rose hips to Terry, who sat at the water's edge leaning against a gravel incline and watching Dahl.

"You should see the size of the bear track we saw," he said to both men. "It's bigger than my mom's roasting pan."

Dahl's eyes grew wide. "Are you going to keep me tied up like this if we run into a bear?"

"Be quiet, Leon. We haven't seen a bear." In his head it sounded like he was talking down a hollow tube and Terry had to control his voice to be certain he didn't shout.

Leon stomped his feet in the wet gravel. "I'm serious. You can't . . ."

"No," Terry cut him off, focusing hard on the prisoner. His voice had a hard edge to it like the devil's club they'd been fighting all day. "You're scared. I'm serious. This is one of those times we talked about, Leon. Now be quiet."

A stiff breeze kicked up as they reached the mine late that afternoon. The sun was on its long downward arc and the wind carried the earthy scent of a distant rain. So far, the sky above them remained clear but things like the weather changed fast in the far north. Terry was shivering noticeably and Kit knew it was imperative to keep him dry.

Thinking of the grizzly tracks, Kit stood at the black mouth of the mine for several seconds, sniffing the air and giving her eyes time to adjust to the dark interior. Air inside the shaft was cool and slightly damp. The flame on Kit's lighter bent toward the darkness ahead, blown by a soft breath of wind that beckoned them inside before disappearing into the far reaches of the cavern. This constant movement kept the air from becoming stale and Kit made a mental note that it might be possible to have a small fire.

On her first trip she hadn't taken the time to explore the mine deeply because of her fear for Terry's health. Now, with the rest of the group standing behind her like an impatient audience waiting for the show to begin, she wished she had. For all she knew a bear or a pack of wolves or worse yet, a lone wolverine had already laid claim to the place. Kit thought again of the huge tracks back by the river, then walked forward a few steps, rifle barrel first. She took a deep breath of the cool air and allowed her fears to ebb. If anything was already living in the mine she would smell it first, even with the breeze coming from behind her. Wolverines in particular seemed to leave their skunky stench on everything they touched. Bears were not much better.

As it turned out the mine smelled like wet earth and sulfur, which probably accounted for why nothing wild had decided to take up residence. The smell of slightly rotten eggs was nothing compared to the motherlode of what the mine provided in a comfortable shelter. There was a sizable support post in the center of the main shaft twenty feet from the entrance. Another twenty feet past that, the main shaft branched out into three smaller shafts. The area between the support post and the offshoot tunnels opened up into a fan-shaped room of sorts about thirty feet across at its widest point. Whoever built the mine had spent a lot of effort and time moving rock. Kit found herself wondering if they'd ever found anything of worth.

Whatever they'd found, the miners had left behind items that were priceless to the weary group. Some light made it in from the mouth of the tunnel. As Paul's eyes adjusted he was able to make out the shape of a dust-covered kerosene lantern on a rough wooden table along the right wall. Closer inspection showed it to have a usable wick. Under the table was a rusty can with the words coal oil printed on the side in flaking white paint. There was no telling how old the stuff was, but when Paul filled up the squeaky lantern, the flame from Kit's lighter easily ignited the old flaxen wick. In the new, relatively brighter light, Paul found a heavy roll of coarse burlap sacking. Hidden away in the darkness of the mine, it was almost like new and would provide serviceable, if scratchy, bedding.

Paul also found a broken pick handle leaning against the cool rock wall. Picking up the sturdy hickory stick like a baseball bat the boy looked at Dahl, now tied to the support post, and frowned. He half-hoped the outlaw would try something so he could save the day.

CHAPTER 19

The Russians grabbed a few hours of sleep Friday night in the hidden 206. Adrik reasoned that no search planes would be out at night and even half-sitting in the small cabin, they slept better than they would have surrounded by mosquitoes. By first light their backs were sufficiently cramped that they were both ready to brave the insects and start for the crash site. Rather than wasting any of the MREs they breakfasted on two cans of apple sauce from the survival duffle.

Adrik had been very careful to get his bearings while still in the air and used the small compass he wore on his watchband to check himself as they traveled. Finding the crash site was not the problem. But knowing where a place is and getting to it across ten odd miles of bug-infested muskeg and patchy forest are two completely different matters.

The tea-colored muck proved to be such a wonderful breeding ground for insects turned the hike into an ordeal even for Adrik. And what was an ordeal for him turned out to be an agonizing torture march for Vasilii Petrov. When the young Russian's low-cut leather shoes weren't being sucked off his feet, he was jumping out of them in fright from the northern pike exploding like hidden mines every few yards in the shallow streams that fed the lake.

It was almost dawn before they reached the small lake with Kit's 180 and even Adrik was exhausted. He took the time to smooth some gravel away from a flat spot in the shade of the spruce trees before laying out his bag. Vasilii, too tired to care about a few stones, rolled his out and climbed inside without looking. In moments the sound of his rattling snores rebounded off the otherwise peaceful lake and chased two loons out for a morning swim to seek a more peaceful secluded location.

Adrik shook his head as he looked at his young employer and listened to the birds fly away on whistling wings. There was no way this man would survive without him in a wilderness like this.

Stress and hard work take there toll even on the mean-hearted, and the sun was high overhead when Adrik stirred in his sleeping bag. He thought he heard the sound of a distant plane and bolted upright with nothing but his head poking out of the drawstring hood. The sound faded and he let himself relax a little. Still, they had to move. Petrov was still asleep and Adrik let him stay that way, happy for the added relief from the man's useless ranting.

He had the sleeping bag tied in a tight roll in a matter of minutes and opened an envelope of pork and rice. It even contained a plastic spoon. He ate the meal cold while he walked around the campsite and studied the remains of the fire. Holding the spoon in his mouth and the food in one hand he knelt and sifted through the ashes. There was nothing. The ground revealed little that he didn't already know from the fly-over.

After the crash, Dahl had been in charge. He'd been the one holding the gun when they flew over. Adrik sucked the pork grease of his spoon and took another bite. Then ... then the girl had turned the tables on him some way. Yes it had to be the girl. The other man was injured and that left only the boy. He left the spoon in his mouth again and clapped a hand against his knee. This girl was incredible.

Vasilii stirred at the noise and woke with the slow, stretching yawn of a lazy teenager with nothing at all to do. His left eye was swollen shut from a mosquito bite, and once half awake, he began to moan about the pain of his face and back. "Have you found their trail yet?" The young Russian was not the least bit embarrassed about having overslept.

"I think so." Adrik threw him one of the MREs; one that said ham and eggs. The stupid man would think he was deferring and giving up the breakfasts but he'd tasted them before. The MREs with eggs in them deserved the name American soldiers gave them—vomlets. Adrik had carefully sorted through the meals and given all the egg dishes to Vasilii, picking out a spaghetti and the only two pork and rice for himself. They were his favorites and usually contained a hard, chocolate-covered cookie.

He used his spoon to point over his shoulder at the dark line of spruce and birch. "There are many animal trails that come down to the lake but I believe I can tell which way they have gone."

Vasilii set aside the pack of gelatinous, slightly green eggs and ripped the top off a pack of thick peanut butter and began to suck out the contents under his bug net. He had a particular fondness for peanut butter. "Well," he said through a thick, sticky mouth. "They better not have taken another swamp. I thought I would lose my feet yesterday, to say nothing of my shoes."

"They left through the forest. Probably to remain hidden from us. Maybe to keep away from these insects." Adrik looked up, as much to keep from having to look at the pitiful sight of Petrov slurping peanut butter as to study the pale, cloud-streaked sky. "That's what I would have done. One of the men is injured and they have taken Dahl as a prisoner. They will have to travel slowly."

"Why would they not just kill him and be done with it?" Vasilii thought out loud as he finished the last of his snack.

"Who can tell about Americans," Adrik shrugged. "They are weak when it comes to killing. It does not come easy for them."

CHAPTER 20

Sunday

There is a belief among elite military survival trainers and men familiar with tough conditions of outdoor living, that the line between civilized and savage is about three days wide. Terry had seen it countless times in Ranger training. The first day out men might throw away the core of an apple—on the third, they would fight over it. In one of the early training exercises each candidate was given a live chicken provided by the local egg company. Along with the chicken, the men were given half a day's rations for a five-day march and told they should expect to live off the land. It would have been much easier on the emotions to kill the chicken right off the bat, but they had food for the first day. In the southern heat the best way to preserve meat was to keep it breathing. By the second day, many of the men made pets out of their birds, talking to them kindly. Some of these trained soldiers even gave their animal a name. But by the fourth day of the march—their third without substantial food, each man killed and ate his feathered companion. It came easier for some than for others. Some carried out the necessity through embarrassed tears but once the meat began to cook each forgot about his lost friend and enjoyed the feast with gusto. On several missions, training and otherwise, Terry, who didn't even particularly care for the feeling of pulp in his orange juice, was reduced to eating insects to keep his belly button from getting too well acquainted with his backbone.

Christina's good cooking had added a greater amount of reserve fuel to his bones than he'd had in the military, but exercise and the martial arts kept him relatively lean. At thirty-six, when many men were sporting a full-size spare tire, Terry McGreggor didn't even have a fifty-mile emergency donut.

Looking around the dim, cave-like atmosphere of the mine, he thought how tasty a few bugs might be at that moment. Seeing none, he leaned back on his rough pallet and told himself it was just his fever talking. Even when he'd been forced to eat them he'd never really craved an insect before.

Dahl sat slumped forward against his ropes in the center of the room, snoring loud, open-mouth snores. Paul slept through the racket the way only an exhausted teenager could, curled in the tattered remnants of his foil blanket and a large square of burlap.

Kit's dark eyes flickered in the orange lantern light; a wild, predatory look in them. The civilized part of her had been cast aside out of necessity. She sat crosslegged, twisting two strands of fine wire into a strangle snare. "How are you feeling?" she whispered, knowing Terry wouldn't tell her the truth.

"Better, after the sleep." His husky voice betrayed him. "How about you?"

"Fine," Kit smiled. "You might say thriving, really. I haven't had the time to make a snare like this since I was Paul's age. But ..." She held up three perfectly twisted wire loops. They were gossamer thin and barely visible in the faint light. "My fingers haven't forgotten how. With any luck we can have a couple of snowshoe hares or spruce hens by evening. It might look like I've got plenty of fat to see me through hard times, but I'm getting hungry."

Terry forced a weak smile making his eyes hurt. "I guess I could eat too. I'm sure Paul's starving." He tried to sit up against the rough wall, wincing at the stab of pain bouncing back and forth from his head to his ribs.

Kit worked with her wire and pretended not to notice. "I

remember my mother chewing willow bark for a headache. Maybe I can find you some."

"We're lucky to have you along." Terry was not a man to show much emotion. It was simply not tactical to give away your feelings, but he felt he owed this woman. If she couldn't save him maybe she could save the boy. "Paul's lucky to have your expertise to guide him in case I don't pull out of this."

Kit blushed in the darkness. The events just past had dredged up many old emotions and she felt uncomfortably exposed. "Don't be silly. You'll be all right." Kit wasn't sure herself about Terry's condition and avoided his eyes while she spoke. "I've sure been impressed with Paul," she said, changing the subject and keeping her voice low so as not to disturb the boy. "You know, I heard him praying last night."

Terry nodded. "He was raised right."

"I can tell. Did you know that even after all he's been through, he prayed that his mother wouldn't worry about him. Can you believe that? I hope I have a son like that someday."

Terry lay back on his lumpy bed and stared up at a grey streak of rock cutting across the ceiling. "I think the pressure of worrying about her is a big part of his problem. Since his father died he's taken it on himself to be man of the house."

Kit let her fingers slide thoughtfully up the long piece of twisted wire. "Well, if he makes it through this, I bet he can handle anything life throws his way. We may be out here a while, you know."

"I've been thinking about that," Terry said turning his head slightly to look up at her. She worked on her snare by feel in the semidarkness, her long black hair hanging loosely around strong shoulders. Her tattered wool clothing was the only thing setting her apart from one of the dioramas he'd seen at the Anchorage museum. "Do you think we're under any kind of a flight path at all out here? It's late in the summer and hunting season should be starting soon, right?"

"I wish I could say yes, but I'm not sure. There might be a few hunters out here in another two weeks but I don't relish waiting that long. Besides, people are pretty sparse up here and the country is so big. Planes go down in these mountains and aren't discovered for years ... if ever." Kit carefully laid her finished snare on top of the other three so they wouldn't tangle. Leaning forward, she wrapped her arms around her legs and rested her chin on her knees. "I need to go get some more water and set these snares. We should start thinking like we might be here for more than a day or two. Even if the Russians give up, we may not see another plane for weeks, especially with late summer storms blowing through here this time of year."

"We need to build some kind of signal fire we can light quickly if we do get a friendly fly over." Terry thought out loud, disgusted at his inability to do the job himself.

"Once I get us some food, I'll work on that."

"Take Paul with you." Terry was able to work into a sitting position and set the pistol in his lap. "I'm okay here with Leon for a while and I don't like the idea of you going out there alone."

"Are you sure?"

"I am," he nodded. "Who knows how I'll feel in a few days and I'm afraid Paul will go crazy cooped up in here." Terry grinned through his pain. "Besides, he likes you. You're easier to talk to—and a lot prettier to boot."

"If you say so." Kit smoothed her ratted hair as best she could. "I was just thinking how much easier my life would be right now if I had a haircut like yours."

The way the mountain dipped and twisted, it was impossible to see what lay around the next bend or behind the next knoll. This was good because it kept the entrance to the mine hidden unless you were right on top of it—a fact which had probably been taken into account by the original miners who wanted to guard their claim. The problem was, the terrain also made it easy to stumble into someone or something before you knew you were right on top of them. Kit didn't want to surprise a napping grizzly but she didn't want to give their positions away to the Russians if they happened to be in the area. In the end, she decided she'd at least have a chance to talk the grizzly out of bad behavior and kept her voice to a whisper, instructing Paul to do the same.

She smelled the waterfall before she heard it and heard it only shortly before she saw it. The cascading stream below it turned out to be an oasis of wood and scrub willow on a mountainside otherwise covered with blueberry shrubs, rock and an occasional dwarf spruce, twisted and canted from blizzard winds. Miner's lettuce and other succulent plants grew lush along the pool at the base of the ten-foot fall and a latticework of dozens of rabbit trails crisscrossed the ground beneath the whiplike willows lining the bank. Closer inspection showed many of the plants had been chewed and nibbled. This would be the perfect place for some of her snares.

Heartened by the prospect of a likely supper, Kit went about setting the wires while Paul looked on and learned. Using nothing for bait, Kit relied on the animal's habit of using the same trail and set her traps in what appeared to be the most popular areas. Twisting the tail of the two-foot wire around the base of a thick branch the size of her thumb, she pulled the thin, almost invisible loop so the tiny twisted eye was held open in a hair trigger noose about ten inches across.

If an unwary bunny were to stick more than his nose through the loop on his way down the trail, the slightest jiggle would cause the noose to tighten and the animal's struggle would quickly end its life.

Kit demonstrated the first one she set by touching it with her finger. Paul was surprised by how quickly the wire circle sprung shut and whistled softly under his breath. "Maybe we should set some of those out for the Russians," he said while Kit reset the trap.

"That's a good idea." She chuckled to herself at the thought. "If we had enough wire. There's enough left for me to teach you how to make these later this evening. I though it might help pass the time if you learned to make a few useful tools."

"That would be way cool." Paul pitched a small round stone from hand to hand while he watched. He enjoyed being with Kit. The idea that she'd grown up in a wilderness like this excited him and he thought he might like to raise his own kids the same way.

Kit looked up from her set and saw him staring at her, deep in thought. Paul was old enough that the silence of the moment made him feel awkward and he looked away, almost dropping the stone. Kit smiled and stood up, arching her back to get the kinks out. "What does that mean on your hat?" She walked uphill a few yards as she spoke and bent to pick a handful of blueberries that carpeted the area.

Watching her, Paul had forgotten he was even wearing a hat, much less what was written on the front and he had to take it off and look. "Oh," he said. "CTR. It's kind of a motto for our church. Choose the Right."

Kit nodded solemnly while she picked. "Words to live by. Strong, solid words, my father would have said.

"Was he an Indian?"

"No. Scottish, but don't hold that against him. He was wise enough." Kit grinned, her smile wide and starkly white against a dirty bronze face. "He was wise enough to marry my mother." Her smile faded into a deeper, secret thought and she sighed, going back to her berry picking. "Choose the Right, eh? I like that." The instant she spoke, her words were punctuated by the explosive drum of wings and two spruce hens erupted from the low berry shrubs beside her.

Both Kit and Paul watched the plump birds settle on the branch of a gnarled little spruce about twenty yards away along the side hill. "We should try to kill them with rocks," Kit said thoughtfully, her mouth watering at the thought of fresh meat. "But they'll probably play us all across the mountain and we'd use more energy catching them than they could give us back."

Paul's face brightened. Without a word he took off at a trot toward the grouse-laden tree. The first rock from his vine maple slingshot hit with such a surprising thump, Paul jumped. The grouse fluttered to the ground in a flurry of wings and loose feathers. Not wanting to lose the precious bird down the steep mountain side, Paul pounced on it quickly, breaking its neck the way he'd seen his father do when he hunted fool's hens back in Montana. His father had always spared him the job of dispatching wounded birds, believing there was no rush to learn that aspect of life.

Surprisingly, the second bird hadn't even moved when her partner fell from the branch beside her. Instead she ducked her head behind a dark clump of needles and black moss, as if not looking at the boy kept her from being seen herself. If they hadn't needed the meat so badly, Paul would have thought the behavior funny. As it was, he considered it a blessing. His aim was better on the second bird and he hit it square in the neck. An instant kill.

With a rush of pride that made his face warm, he picked up both birds by their feet and carried them back to Kit who smiled in quiet approval.

"You have saved us all from a hungry night," she said,

admiring the two fat birds. "I think I should give you an Athabascan name for that."

Paul beamed. He wondered if he should take his hat off for such a bestowal. He decided it would be best, just in case. "Is Kit your Athabascan name?"

"No, that's just a nick name. My mother gave me my Indian name when I was five. *Chekesillik.* It means long, silky hair.'"

"That's a good one." Paul let out a reverent breath at what seemed to be such personal information. "It fits you."

"Thank you. Now let's see ..." Kit looked hard at Paul for so long he began to fidget.

"Should I tell other people my Athabascan name?" he asked, to break the uneasy silence.

Kit shrugged, but continued to study him. "That's up to you. It's no secret but I only tell mine to people I trust not to make fun of it." She raised an eyebrow at a sudden inspiration and put a hand on Paul's shoulder. "I think your name is *Zho Gezell.* Little wolf. It was the name of my favorite lead dog when I was growing up. Many times he saved my skin with his bravery on the trail and like you he always tried to choose the right way to get us home."

"*Zho Gezell,*" Paul whispered. "I like it."

"I'm glad." Kit gathered up her shirt full of berries and the full water bottles. "Now, Little Wolf, let's go back and show Terry what you have got us for supper."

She didn't tell Paul the other reason she'd chosen that particular name. Even in the happiness of his successful hunt a dangerous fire burned in the young man's eyes—the wild fire of a young, angry wolf that threatened to consume him and all around him if he let it.

There is no seasoning more savory than true hunger. There was no pepper or salt for the meat, but the roasting birds flavored the air better than the finest Thanksgiving turkey stuffed full of sage dressing. With the constant breeze coming from the mouth of the mine, Kit reasoned that the smoke would be carried back into the shaft to whereever the wind took it, perhaps out a different entrance or a crack in the rock further up the mountain. So far, her theory had worked and what little smoke her tiny fire created disappeared into the blackness of the mine. As a precaution she used only the driest wood she could find and kept the birds beside the coals instead of over them to keep their drippings from smoking up the room.

The dancing light from the fire raised Terry's spirits some. Kit gave him a handful of willow bark along with most of the fresh berries, but he was too exhausted to eat them. He'd gone downhill almost immediately on their return as if he'd been staying alert to guard Dahl by willpower alone. The shirttail bandage Kit had made him had fallen off. It was so filthy and encrusted with blood it couldn't be used again. Kit wanted to use another piece of her shirt but found it was almost as dirty as the old bandage. His fever had grown so bad that even with the added warmth of the fire, Terry was wracked with chills. The area around the wound on his head was red and swollen. He'd already put the pistol under the burlap so Dahl, who'd been eyeing him all afternoon wouldn't be tempted by it. It took every ounce of energy he had not to give in to the mixture of pain and fever sapping his will and causing the flickering interior of the mine to wobble back and forth like a child's teeter-totter. As soon as he was aware the others were back he let himself fall into a shivering stuporous doze.

Dahl's eyes played around the room, darting from person to person but lingering on the dripping meat. "How about giving me some of those berries?" he said, opening up his bound palms. If whining had a gesture, that was it.

Kit looked up from where she squatted, tending the sizzling grouse. Paul's eyes sparkled with barely controlled anger.

"No," Kit said and went back to her cooking.

Leon leaned back with a moan and beat his head against the support beam in self-pity, bringing a fine shower of dirt down on his head from the ceiling. "Are you gonna let me starve to death?" He spat to get the dust out of his mouth. "I don't see why he should get all the berries." The prisoner's demeanor changed in a flash and he leaned forward, looking hard at Paul. "Come on kid," he said in the same voice he would have used if he were untied and giving the orders. "Give me some of those berries." It was the wrong thing to say.

Paul glared and his head began to twitch in anger. "You better shut up, mister." His voice came out more of a screech than he wanted it to but it couldn't be helped. "You're bigger than I am, but if you weren't I'd have killed you by now..." Paul looked at his friend shivering on the ground, then turned back to Dahl. His mouth twisted cruelly as he spoke. "If he dies, I plan to kill you no matter how big you are." The boy held the broken pick handle like a ball bat and for an instant looked like he intended to use it.

A heavy, almost suffocating feeling filled the mine during the confrontation and Terry stirred, sensing the mood even through his fever.

"Paul." His voice was a chattering croak. "Would you bring me a sip of that water please?"

The boy's head snapped around and the hatred of the moment drained from his face when he thought about taking care of Terry.

"I'd never correct you in front of the prisoner if I could help it," Terry whispered as Paul helped him get a drink from one of the water bottles. "But think about what you're saying."

Paul hung his head. "I would kill him if I had to."

Terry squinted from the pain of swallowing. "I know you would, Paul. For your sake I hope you don't have to. If something happens to me I want you and Kit to walk away. Leave him a water bottle and walk away. But don't kill him out of anger. I promise you it would eat you up inside." Terry coughed and fell back, exhausted from such a long speech. "It smells like that grouse you got us is about ready. Maybe it will give me some energy. I want you to give some to Dahl too."

"But ..."

Terry tapped his forefinger weakly on the boy's arm. "We're lawmen, son and we have a responsibility. You run on now and help Kit."

When the juice ran clear from the cooking grouse, Kit removed them from the fire. She'd opened them up butterfly fashion and skewered them on peeled willow branches. Once the birds were cooked it was an easy matter for her to run her knife up the back of each and split them into two fairly equal portions. "Take this to Terry," She said giving Paul one of the larger halves still stuck on a sharpened willow. The warm smell of the roasted meat brought a series of growls and rumbles from her empty stomach. She half-agreed with Paul about Dahl. It was his fault they were hungry. But she knew Terry was right. Taking the stick with half of the smallest bird, she walked to Dahl and handed it to him without speaking.

Leon's hunger so consumed him, he tore at the steaming meat

without caring that it burned his mouth and hands. Fear of being caught and tortured by Petrov and the cramping humiliation of being held prisoner had used up all his strength and most of his sense. He wouldn't have cared if the meat was on fire. It was food and he needed it. He ripped into the meat with such gusto that he nearly cracked a tooth on a piece of broken thigh bone. Slowly, trying not to draw too much attention to himself, he lowered the meat to his lap and studied the bone he'd just exposed. It was small, about as big around as a pencil and no longer than a toothpick, but it was broken off sharp and jagged on the end where it connected to the bird's miniature drumstick.

A weapon. Leon's heart beat wildly and he resumed gnawing at the meat. Partly to get every morsel from his small portion, but mostly to free the broken thigh bone so he could hide it before Kit took the carcass away. It surprised him that he hadn't thought about it before and he cursed himself for being so slow-witted. Of course the grouse would have bones. He'd been watching for a way to escape since the crash site but with the marshal in the mix it was too risky. Now, with the lawman obviously not much of a problem, Dahl knew all he needed to do was get out of the ropes and he would be in charge again. The luck of finding the sharp bone filled him with as much warmth as the meager meal and he found he had to concentrate to keep a smug look off his face. He smiled inside himself at the fickle nature of life. One minute these three idiots had him tied to a post begging for a handful of berries and the next he'd have all the food he wanted; all because of a tiny grouse bone no bigger than his little finger.

Leon marveled at his good fortune and stared through the darkness at Paul. The stupid kid had even been so bold as to threaten his life. The outlaw tucked the lucky find under his knee. It wouldn't be too long now and he would show them all who would kill who.

CHAPTER 21

Though Skip Garret was not what could be termed a great conversationalist, it was a rare occasion when he couldn't think of at least some little thing to talk about and pass the time. Worry for Terry and Paul mixed with his aversion to flying chewed on whatever part of his brain it was that helped him speak, and he sat mute in the back of the Super Cub for most of the morning, trying to keep down the two pieces of dry toast he'd eaten for breakfast.

His sleep had been fitful the night before and he half-expected a visit from Rockwell to tell him everything would be all right. Mac had invited him to dinner, but he declined. The last thing his stomach wanted after a day of bouncing through the Yukon skies was food. Kate's home cooking over the last several months had insured that he had plenty of reserve calories and it didn't hurt him to miss a meal or two.

Sunday was no more than a rehash of Saturday evening. They would fly for three hours on one of the grids, Roberson swooping down like a hawk on field mouse when he saw something that caught his attention. On each dive, Skip braced himself for the crash he knew was inevitable. About the time Skip knew he could stand no more, the Mountie would announce he needed more fuel and return to the ranch just in the nick of time for a bathroom break and ten minutes of Skip trying to get his stomach back where it belonged.

Every minute that ticked by added a layer of worry and both men went the entire day without saying so much as ten words to each other. Mac set the Super Cub down on the gravel strip at the ranch when it was too dark to search effectively.

"You're welcome to come over, ya know," the Mountie said. He was smiling but the strain was beginning to show on even his benign face. "I can cook us up something that will settle your stomach, eh."

"Thank you, but I think I'll pass." Skip realized the Mountie wanted to be friendly but he was too tired to spend any more time with anyone. "I think a little solitary time with the horses might clear my head." He stuck out his hand. "I do appreciate it, though."

A call to Kate on the ranch phone made Skip more depressed than ever. If he'd only had some news to tell her for Christina and Terry. That would have been something. As it was, there was not much to say besides he missed her and couldn't wait to get home. The baby was still kicking like crazy. Never one for lengthy telephone conversations, Skip said his I-love-you-and-good-bye in a matter of minutes.

The chilly, night air around the corrals was heavy with the smell of dust and hay. These were familiar smells to Skip and he took a deep breath to calm his nerves. Putting one boot on the bottom rail of the fence, he rested his arms and head on the top. One of the few remaining horses coughed in the shadows.

"Where are you, partner?" Skip sighed under his breath. He was not one to cry but his stomach was in knots and his whole body felt heavy with worry. Deep down, he knew something was very wrong. He stared into the darkness. "Where are you?"

Skip was too tired to jump when he heard Porter's voice beside him. He'd been surprised when the old gunfighter hadn't come earlier.

"No luck?" The old man settled himself on the top rail of the fence and smiled softly down at his friend.

"None," Skip said, still staring into the night.

"Well, they're still alive. Maybe you'll find them tomorrow."

Skip looked up, tipping his hat back on his head. "Forgive me for asking, Port, but could you just give me a clue about which way to look?"

"I wish I could." The old gunfighter scratched his chin under the flowing white beard. "Truth is I don't know myself. What I mean to say is, I can get to him, but I don't know how to tell you to get to him. You see, those of us that are unencumbered with bodies move around a little different than you more earthly types. I'm truly sorry, but it makes it nigh to impossible to give directions."

Skip looked away again. "Couldn't hurt to ask."

"Don't be so glum, boy," Rockwell said, hopping down on the ground. "I'll be close to you tomorrow, watching out for you like I promised. I have faith in you, even if you don't—and I know Brother McGreggor does."

By Sunday afternoon Adrik was beginning to grow a tiny doubt. They'd been wandering about these thick woods for almost three days, dodging all manner of insects and low-flying search planes without so much as a clue as to where Dahl and the others had gone. He had been sure he was going in the right direction when they left the crash site, then on some rocky ground all sign of tracks disappeared. They had walked on most of the day, zigzagging in the hope they would find something to point them in the right direction.

Vasilii was becoming a danger to himself, he whined so, and Adrik was on the verge of shooting him by the time they stopped for a bite of lunch in a small clearing. They had already eaten most of the MREs but saved a bit of the fruitcake and two cookies. Adrik made up his mind that if they didn't find Dahl before nightfall, he would kill Vasilii and take his cookie. He had the rifle and was sure he could hunt game, but taking the cookie would solve two problems at once: hunger and Petrov's whining.

Vasilii noticed the change in Adrik's behavior and stayed behind the larger man much of the time, unwilling to turn his back. He'd just torn the foil top off his slice of fruitcake when he heard a rattle in the brush beside him and then a grunt. The Russian smiled when a baby moose emerged from the trees on long, almost comical legs. In his country it would have been called an elk. He extended his hand, offering it some fruitcake. "Come here little fellow, you look like you might have some juicy steaks on ..." Before Petrov could finish, a louder grunt, followed by a much larger moose erupted from the bramble behind the baby.

The cow's black hackles stood straight up like a porcupine as she pawed the leafy ground not ten feet from the petrified Russian. She grunted again and her calf obediently ambled off into the trees. Without warning the cow rose up on her hind legs pawing in front of her with sharp black hooves. Broken from his trance, Petrov dropped his fruitcake and whirled in his tracks, running for the safety of a thick group of spruce. The moose ignored Adrik who remained motionless until she trotted after Vasilii. The dark Russian followed, but not too quickly. He wanted to see what happened.

Petrov crashed wildly through the trees, dodging this way and that, paying no heed to the devil's club that tore at the skin of his arms and legs. The cow moose stayed right on his heels, determined to chase him completely away from her baby and stomp him to jelly if he gave her the chance. The trees were all that saved him but he was running so fast he ran out of them before he could do anything about it.

All at once the terrain changed from heavy forest to open plain with low willow and scrub—and not much to hide behind. Vasilii could hear the hoofbeats of the moose getting closer behind him and looked around wildly for a place to hide. The forest had disappeared behind him and there was nothing but hills as far as the eye could see.

The cow hit him hard with her huge, bony head and sent him flying into a wispy stand of willows. She had been running so fast, she went right by him and had to turn in order to come back and finish him off. Turning her head back and forth to bring her target into focus, the giant animal rose up again on her hind legs.

A single shot to her head from Adrik's rifle dropped her where she stood and she landed in a crumpled heap, her large bulbous nose not two feet from a trembling Petrov.

"I thought you were going to let her trample me to death," the panting Russian said, trying to rise on wobbly legs.

"I did not want to risk shooting you," Adrik lied. In fact, he was going to let the moose do the killing for him until he noticed the mountains to the southwest. He'd been ready to let Petrov die and be done with this whole affair. Then, he saw the smoke. High on one of the foothills, an almost invisible plume snaked toward the evening sky. He realized he might need Petrov after all to take care of Dahl while he hunted the Indian girl. So he shot the moose.

The baby walked into the clearing and over to its dead mother, nosing her gently. "Shoot it as well," Vasilii screamed. He had suddenly developed a severe hatred of moose.

"No, I do not want to risk someone hearing another shot. Besides, the young one will make a bear or other wild beast some good sport." Adrik stared at the distant mountains. "I know where they are now," he said as much to himself as Petrov.

"Where?" Vasilii rubbed his sore back and looked around, seeing nothing.

"I see their fire. It is yet a long way off, but we will reach them by tomorrow and you can have what you want from that fool Dahl."

Both men quickened their pace. They had to go back for the gear left behind before the moose incident, but with a sure direction to follow even backtracking didn't dampen their spirits. Vasilii looked everywhere for the piece of fruitcake he'd offered to the baby moose, but he never found it. He couldn't have known that while he ran for his life, Adrik had taken the time to scoop up the precious food and stuff it into his own mouth. He had just swallowed the last of it when he shot the cow.

For now, Vasilii chased his hunger away with thoughts of regaining his father's two million dollars and the terrible justice he'd planned for the stupid American.

CHAPTER 22

Monday

"So," Skip said, trying to adjust the green headset so it didn't squeeze the brains out of his head. He and Mac had been searching for a day and a half and seen nothing more than a dozen moose and half again as many woodland caribou. He talked to ease the monotony. "What's the deal with you Canadians not letting me bring my pistol up here anyway?"

Roberson shrugged and threw Skip a quick look over his shoulder. "We have strict handgun laws up here—no tolerance for that sort of thing, eh." He offered the deputy a bit of Macintosh toffee as a peace offering at the talk of such a delicate subject.

Skip declined the candy. "Tell me about it," he said, staring out the window at the endless landscape beneath him.

The Mountie banked the plane sharply to check out a thick copse of gold-leafed birch trees, nearly causing Skip to lose the protein bar he'd nibbled for lunch. "I know you Americans think differently than we do about your handguns but think of it this way. During prohibition, when liquor was legal in Canada, would you have let it cross into the States just for a special occasion?"

" I don't drink."

"That's not the point." Seeing nothing in the trees, Roberson began straight and level flight again, allowing Skip's stomach to settle a little. "Maybe it's not a perfect analogy, but if you were going to China or France you'd accept it if they wouldn't let you bring your gun, wouldn't you?"

"I suppose so." Skip nodded. "But I'd still gripe about it."

"Well Canada is as much of a different country as they are." Mac gave a good-hearted chuckle and shook his head. "Sometimes you Americans forget that Canada's not just another big state to the north."

The small plane buffeted like a truck with bad shocks on a wagon road. "Better tighten your safety belt," Roberson said, settling low in his seat. His voice was grim. "We have a few clouds moving in and some bumps are inevitable. This is going to make searching nearly impossible."

Already, pockets of wispy white clouds hung in pools over the landscape below them reducing the land they could search to a patchwork of visible area. "I can try to get below the clouds for a while and fly the terrain but by noon we'll be … " Roberson held up his hand as another unfamiliar voice came across the radio. It was Chuck Demming.

"Hey Mackenzie, you on the radio?" The voice was smooth and matter-of-fact, the easy-going voice of a relaxed bush pilot.

"Go ahead Chuck." Roberson pulled back on the stick to gain altitude and improve radio reception.

"I think we got your wreckage here in Loon lake. I can see the wing of a yellow Cessna— Mac, the plane's in the water, but it looks like someone built a fire on the beach."

Roberson and Skip had been holding their breath and each let out a sigh of relief at the mention of a fire. The Mountie turned his Super Cub into a steep bank, increasing power for optimum speed. He didn't care what was below him now.

They reached Loon lake in less than twenty minutes. Mac shuddered when he saw the battered hulk of Kit's plane hanging in the deep green water like a dead fish. He'd been a passenger in the little yellow Cessna many times, though Kit had rarely let him fly it. As a pilot, it gave him pause whenever he saw any plane after a crash, but seeing Kit's plane torn apart made him sick with worry.

The remains of a fire were clearly visible as they overflew the long gravel shore, but there was no sign of life. "We'd better go get a chopper and come back to investigate." Skip said, pressing his nose to the window, searching for any sign of Terry and Paul.

"No need for that," Roberson said, bringing his nimble aircraft around in an arcing loop. "This looks Super Cubable." To Skip's horror he cut the power and pointed the plane toward the narrow gravel beach.

Roberson extended full flaps and the light, fabric-covered Piper settled toward the grey strip of earth between the line of black spruce and blue-green water. The beach was wide enough to allow both of the plane's fat tundra wheels to stay out of the water—but not by much. The propeller threw up a shower of white spray as the stall-warning buzzer squealed like a sick duck and they touched down in a series of rolling thumps. Skip stared past the Mountie's shoulders at the dark line of trees that waited at the end of the beach, bracing himself for what he thought was certain impact.

When Skip felt sure he'd be having spruce trees for lunch, Roberson brought the plane to a halt. Skip found he'd been unconsciously pressing against the floor in an effort to assist in stopping the plane and both legs had the tingling feeling of adrenaline he always got after a fight.

Mac gunned the engine and turned the plane around, taxiing back toward the remains of the fire.

"Looks pretty barren," Skip observed, unfolding himself from the cramped back seat. Being back on steady ground coupled with the relief of getting closer to his friends made him light-headed.

"It's not like Kit to leave the crash site like this." Roberson looked up at Skip from where he studied the fire and grinned. "Not that she crashes all the time mind you, it's just standard procedure to stay put until you're found." The relief of finding any sign that his fiance was alive left the stoic young Mountie feeling a little giddy.

"I understand what you meant," Skip said scanning the area around the fire. He felt sure Terry would leave him some kind of sign—if he was able. The sudden thought hit him in the face like a three-pound sledge hammer. There was nothing to say they all made it to shore after the crash. For all he knew one or more of them were still strapped into the sunken airplane only a few yards away.

"Look at this." Roberson retrieved a crumpled piece of paper from the dead coals. It was partially burned but most of the words were still readable. "We want only your prisoner ... Run with him and we make no promises," the Mountie read aloud. He took a plastic evidence baggie out of his shirt pocket and carefully placed the note inside. "Your prisoner," he mused to himself.

"That's good news," Skip slapped a hand on his thigh. "Terry must have Leon Dahl in custody."

Roberson nodded, his mind working to process the new information. "The Russian boys wouldn't be able to land poor Swensen's 206 on this puny lake, eh ... not with Kit's plane taking up so much room anyway. I'm trying to think where the next nearest spot would be for them to set down."

Skip felt that familiar prickle on the back of his neck and strained his eyes around the dark woods behind him. "They may have been here and gone already." He shook his head at the number of game trails leading from the trees to the water's edge. "I sure wish I'd paid more attention to what Terry tried to teach me about ..." Skips voice trailed off and he cocked his head to the side, a wide grin forming under his mustache.

"About what?" Roberson frowned at the man's quizzical behavior.

"About tracking." Skip stopped at the base of a tall white birch about as big around as his leg and pointed to the carving. "I knew you'd leave me a message, old buddy," he whispered under his breath."

"Gen. 1917," Roberson read the letters carved deep into the powdery, paper-like bark. He'd often cited young lovers around Dawson for carving their initials into the local trees in much the same manner. Of course, he'd been appalled when Kit carved KT loves MR inside a heart on the biggest birch in the city park. It took everything he had to keep from lecturing her about it, but he was smart enough to know Kit didn't respond well to lectures. Still, out of good conscience he let off the next three couples he caught doing the very same thing with nothing more than a stern warning.

"Do you understand what it means?"

"Sure do, "Skip traced the outline of the letters and tried to guess what his friend was thinking when he carved them. It's a Bible verse from the Old Testament: Genesis chapter 19, verse 17, where the Lord is warning Lot to scoot out of Sodom. Terry and I used to have a friend that referred us to this particular scripture when we got too wound up with things at work and needed to get away. Sort of his secret signal to us that we were getting too edgy for our own good. "*... look not behind thee, neither stay thou in all the plain; escape to the mountain lest thou be consumed.*" The land's pretty flat around here, but weren't there some mountains off to the west?"

Roberson scratched his chin thoughtfully. "Flee to the mountains, eh? That would be just like Kit. She grew up in the shadow of the Brooks Range. There are some fair-sized mountains a few miles west of here. They could have started for them, I suppose. You can't see them from here for all the trees, but Kit would know they're there."

"That's it then." Skip pounded the carved birch with his fist. "We've finally got something to work with." A stiff wind whipped off the surface of the lake and caught him full in the face. "And none too soon. I don't think we'd be able to see much from up there with all this weather moving in."

Roberson cocked his head upward and watched a procession of silver-grey clouds roll across the sky like soldiers marching in rank, only to pile up into a stormy mess on the southern horizon.

"The mountains are less than ten miles away as the crow flies so they should have made it by now. Let's get back in the air and head that direction to see what we can find. I wouldn't worry about the weather, this could easily blow over."

Skip shook his head at the thought of rejoining the rolling clouds, but the idea of finding Terry and Paul buoyed him up. Better to get back in the Cub's seat quickly while he was still happy about their find. He was happy to be going in the right direction, but Skip still could not stop the nagging feeling in his gut that told him things weren't quite the way they should be with Terry and Paul. "Okay." He turned his back on the tree and started toward the Super Cub. "Let's get going then. We're close. I can feel it."

The takeoff was far worse than the landing in that Skip had more time to think about it. Roberson knew he'd have to use every inch of beach to take off and clear the trees at the other end. Skip's confidence went right out the window when the Mountie pulled the tail of the little plane backward by hand until it was almost in the trees to give him the longest runway possible. Opening the throttle until Skip thought the little plane would rattle apart, Roberson didn't let off the brakes until he had the flaps set for a short field takeoff and full power. When he did release the shaking plane it fairly jumped off the makeshift runway. Roberson struggled with the control stick in the gusty wind, trying to climb as quickly as he could without causing a stall. To Skip, it looked like he was aiming them straight for the line of trees. Skip swore he could hear the fat tundra tires scrape the tree tops as they overflew them.

Roberson kept the throttle open and headed for the long green and gold line of mountains that became visible as soon as they cleared the spruces around the lake. "You up here Chuck?" he said into the radio.

There was a crackle of static in the headphones. "I'm here. Did you find em?"

"Negative on that, but we think we know where they're going. They left a note of sorts that said they may be heading for the mountains west of here. Could you lend us a hand concentrating the search over that way?"

There was a pause on the other end that said Demming didn't have good news. "I still have enough fuel to help you for a few minutes but we're having multiple lightning strikes to the south of us and I'm going to have to send Frenchy and Jim to check them out as long as your folks are well enough to leave a note. Phil Waterton's bird came down with a bad case of carburetor flu about an hour ago so he's out of the picture." It was a hard decision but one that had to be made. There were only so many pilots to go around and the lightning strikes had to be checked out for possible wildfires.

"Roger that, Chuck. I understand. Things are getting bumpy up here. If the clouds keep piling up we're not going to be able to do much mountain flying anyway. Appreciate your help."

Skip hardly even listened to the radio conversation. Almost a thousand feet below, strung out next to the silver ribbon of a creek was Bull Witherspoon's camp. Lines of clean white tents sat in two neat rows facing each other with a communal fire and eating area in between. Bull was known far and wide for his tidy camps. At the east end of the camp, about fifty yards from the nearest tent was a makeshift rope corral that held the groups horses. The pack mules, who stayed married to their horses, grazed nearby, presumably hobbled, though it was impossible to tell from Skip's vantage point.

"Do you think you could set down near that camp?" Skip pointed out the side window when Roberson looked back at him.

"Why, are you ill?"

"No. Think about it, though. We're a few minutes away from getting grounded by the weather anyway, right?"

Roberson shrugged. "Very possible."

"Witherspoon has horses we could borrow. I don't relish the idea of quitting the search when we're this close to finding them."

The Mountie took a deep breath and looked at the line of wrinkled peaks in the distance. Clouds already obscured the higher faces and any sort of mountain flying would be tricky if not down right suicidal. "All right then. Get a good lay of the land while we're aloft. I'm not a hundred percent familiar with the terrain around here from the ground, eh. I'm not suggesting that I'll get lost, but there are a lot of bogs and such so it could well be slow going on the flat." He swung the Super Cub in a slow descending circle overflying a smooth, relatively treeless gravel bar on the far side of the camp from the horses. There were no large trees to contend with and compared to their landing strip at the crash site, this barren plain seemed to have enough room to land a jetliner. After a low pass to check for any obstructions, the plane settled onto the bumpy gravel wash and was stopped in a matter of moments.

The visiting plane raised no small commotion in the nearby camp and before Roberson could unlatch his door he was greeted by three middle-aged Japanese men with video cameras who had taped the entire approach and landing. As soon as Belle realized who it was in the plane, she ran as fast as her stub legs could carry her and bounded at Skip's feet like a Pogo stick gone haywire. In fact, the dog lavished so much attention on him Skip began to get a little embarrassed in front of all the reserved Japanese. *"Boku no inu desu,"* Skip said by way of explanation when he bent over to scratch her behind the ears and she smothered his face in sloppy kisses—it's my dog.

"Ahhhhh," the Japanese men said. One, wearing a floppy green L.L. Bean fishing hat continued to video the happy reunion while the other two bowed deeply to Skip. A slender man of about fifty with the craggy face of a mountaineer smiled and said something about what a fine master Skip was to hunt all over the Yukon in an airplane for his lost dog.

Skip started to explain, but realized it had been almost fifteen years since his mission to Japan and "this is my dog" was stretching the limits of his ability to explain things beyond "Hello, I'm fine, how are you?" So, instead he asked: *"Witherspoon san wa doko desu ka?"* Where's Mr. Witherspoon? The man in the floppy hat pointed toward a large cook tent but kept filming as he did.

Roberson look quizzically at Skip and scratched his head. "Japanese, eh? I had you figured a little differently."

"Yeah, well ..." Skip was about to say there was a lot the Mountie didn't know about him but decided it sounded a little too cocky. "I was a church missionary over there for a while." He shrugged. "It comes in handy. You never know when you might run into a bunch of Japanese tourists when you're on an investigation out in the middle of the Yukon Territory."

Roberson continued to look at Skip with a smiling eye. "I suppose not."

"Skiparoo!" Bull Witherspoon emerged from a large canvas cook tent in the center of camp wearing a white apron and brandishing a ten-inch butcher knife. The wind had kicked up and he used his free hand to keep the long apron from blowing up in his face. "I figured when I heard the plane coming over it might be you interrupting my pork roast. What's up? If I know you, you're coming to steal my best horses." The man pointed the sharp knife at the two lawmen accusingly.

Skip laughed out loud and took out his comb. "Why, sure we did, Bull." He combed through his mustache while he talked. "You know how much I hate to fly. You don't aim to protect them from us with that knife do you? The Mountie here is the only one armed. He wouldn't allow me a handgun in his country."

"And it's a good thing he doesn't. If you were armed, who knows what you'd be stealin' from a poor taxpayer like me." Bull threw the knife point first into the wooden top of a camp table where it stuck with a resounding thunk, much to the delight of his onlooking Japanese guests. The packer wiped his hands on the apron and shook hands with Skip and Roberson. "So what's the news of your friends?"

The Mountie brought him up to speed, then Skip said: "So you see why we could use a couple of your horses. We're awfully close, Bull. I don't want a storm to make them wait another day. Beyond that, there are outlaws in this mix and I don't want them to get there before we do."

Witherspoon scratched his whiskered cheek. "You're right Skip, you need to get to them fast, but I gotta be honest with you. I know what kind of horseman you are and all, but this really ain't the most forgiving horse country around here. If you don't watch out you can end up in a bog up to your elbows with your mount still underneath you."

"I thought about that," Roberson said. "I know this area a little, Mr. Witherspoon, and I feel sure I can keep us out of the swamps. I remember a moraine nearby here that should take us at least as far as the base of the mountains. Then we shouldn't have to contend with the muskeg."

"No, you'll just have to contend with outlaws and bears trying to kill my horses." Bull walked in between the men patting each on the back and herding them with him as he walked toward the horses. "I guess I should quit slowin' you down and let you be on your way." He pointed with an open hand to the portable electric fence where he kept his animals confined. "The only two horses of any account I have are Raven and Havoc—that rangy black and the black and white paint over there. Other than those two, all I got is dude ponies and any of them would hightail it back here every time you let slack in the reins." He looked Skip in the eye. "You know you're welcome to whatever you need, Skipper. All my guests have sore behinds anyway and could use a day off."

Skip looked at Roberson who nodded in approval. "Thanks Bull, I appreciate it."

"You'll be compensated for the use of the animals, Mr. Witherspoon," Roberson assured him already taking a saddle from the nearby tarp and walking toward Raven, the coal-black horse.

"Oh, I know I will," Witherspoon grinned. "But I don't need any money. I got a couple of meanhearted mules here that need their shoes reset. When Skip gets his friends rescued and the bad guys put away, he can come back and see to them. Right Skip?"

"Whatever you say, Bull," Skip groaned, tightening the cinch on the tall paint horse. His ribs screamed at the prospect of bending over to shoe a rank mule.

When he finished tacking up, Roberson swung easily onto his horse and trotted back to his plane. Dismounting, but still holding the reins, he rummaged behind the back seat and pulled out a pump action 12-gauge shotgun and a tube of insect repellent. Swinging back into the saddle he rode up next to Skip and offered the gun to him with a proud smile. "I'm truly sorry about you not having a handgun. Since there is no law saying you can't have a shotgun, you should have this in case I have to make an arrest."

"You mean in case we have to make an arrest." Skip cocked his head, but took the shotgun anyway.

"Not technically. If anyone comes into custody, it will be in Canadian custody."

Witherspoon chuckled and slapped the paint on its rump causing it to lunge forward a step. "You boys best stop arguing and get on the trail." The packer turned to walk back to the cook tent and his waiting pork roast, then turned as if struck with an afterthought. "One more thing, Skip. That Havoc horse you're riding didn't get his name from being a pussycat. Seems like one time a ride at least, he takes it on hisself to test my riding skill. It could be first rattle outta the box or it could be when I'm least expecting it. But mark my words, he'll blow up on you at least one time before the ride's over. If he hasn't bucked and he sees you're about done, you best watch out. He feels it's his sworn duty." Witherspoon pulled the butcher knife out of the table and winked at Skip. "Anyhow, I just thought you might want to know."

CHAPTER 23

By late morning Terry's teeth chattered uncontrollably from fever. In his present condition, Kit didn't want to leave him alone with Dahl who'd grown strangely smug over the last few hours. They needed more water, and she thought she might be able to find some medicinal plants her mother had taught her to use as a poultice. Most importantly, she knew if they stood any chance of being rescued, she would need to build a signal fire. With the scarcity of any wood along the mountainside, let alone good dry wood, it would need to be one large fire she could start quickly.

She mused on the problem all morning, while she gave the last sips of water to Terry and listened to everyone's bellies growl for more grouse. Their stomachs had shrunk so much from lack of food that the small pieces of roasted grouse had come close to filling them up the night before. Small stomachs didn't need as much food, but they needed to be fed often to stay happy and low rumbling fairly echoing in the close quarters of the mine told her it was feeding time.

She poured the last few drops of water from one of the water bottles on a rag torn from her filthy shirt and laid across Terry's forehead. Steam rose from the wet cloth into the cool air. Paul said nothing but it was easy to see the worry in the lines on his brow; lines that shouldn't be there for another twenty years. He looked at Kit with pleading in his eyes, smart enough to know she was their only hope. Terry's only hope.

"You stay here and guard Leon," Kit didn't try to keep the conversation a secret from the prisoner. Whispering seemed to her to be a sign of weakness. She wanted him to hear. To know at least part of her plan. "Keep the pick handle with you, Paul. If he tries to get up hit him as hard as you can across the knees. Do you understand?"

Paul stared at the frowning outlaw and nodded slowly. His look almost dared the man to try something.

"Okay then." Kit gathered up the empty water bottles and started to get up. Terry's eyes fluttered open and he licked his dry lips, cracked from the high fever. He opened his mouth to speak but no words came out. Kit took his shivering hand in hers. "I'm going to go get a signal fire ready." She couldn't tell whether he understood her or not. The peaceful, hollow expression in his eyes reminded her of her uncle—her mother's brother— the day before he died. He had known the end was near and once he accepted it his eyes had taken on the same focusless gaze Terry's had. Still, she wanted to explain to him what she was doing, if only to understand it better herself.

"I'm going to check the snares and get us more food and water. I've been thinking of some plants that might help with your infection. I should be back in a little while."

Terry's eyes fluttered again and he squeezed her hand to show that he understood before lapsing back into a shaky sleep. She set his hand gently back on his chest and rose to her feet with a groan. As she grabbed the rifle and walked toward the mouth of the mine and the muted light of day, she thought she heard Leon chuckle softly to himself. It was an evil, hateful giggle sending a shiver up her spine and made her turn around and fear for Paul. The boy waved at her in the twilight of the room. "I'll be fine," he said. "Be careful, we need you."

Kit wanted the signal fire to be close enough to the mine she could light it quickly, but separated enough so the Russians wouldn't know where they were hiding if they found the fire. After searching the area between the waterfall and their hiding spot, she decided on a jutting ledge beside the waterfall and thirty feet above the willow-lined stream where she'd set her snares. The mine was nearby, only a hundred or so yards away and she figured at the run, she or Paul could get from there to the fire in less than a minute. The problem would be to build a fire that would start quickly. She looked up at the gathering clouds and shivered. It would have to start even if it was damp. Through the willows, across the shallow creek was a small bowl in the mountainside containing a pocket of birch trees. It was hard, backbreaking work dragging what deadwood she could find first across the face of the hill, then across the creek, and finally up the steep outcropping to where she wanted to put her signal. Since she had no axe, Kit concentrated on wood no bigger around than her wrist. It was easier to break and would start better anyway. After almost an hour she had a crisscross stack about as high as her waist that looked like a white-skinned log cabin in need of chinking. She filled the center with frizzed strips of dry, paper-like bark she'd torn from the bigger birch trees and as many dead willows as she could find.

She stepped back and sat on the ground to admire her work. The tower of wood seemed tall enough to do the trick and the willows should smoke enough to bring a search plane around. To get it all started, she would need a flame; a strong, dependable flame that wouldn't blow out in the wind. The wind was one of the main reasons Kit chose the high escarpment. It would help fan the flames and get the fire going quickly once it was ignited—but first it had to be ignited.

Spreading a curl of birch bark about the size of her hand on the ground at her knees, Kit took the magnesium fire starter she always carried when she flew, out of her pocket and began to shave thin silver shavings into a pile. Since she feared there might be only one chance, she spent a considerable amount of time working on the flammable shavings until she had used almost a quarter of the rod. Once hit with a spark, the magnesium would burn relatively quickly but it would be white hot and catch anything around it—even damp tinder, Kit hoped.

After she slid the shavings under the other bits of frizzed bark and willow, she took the pencil flare from her pocket and laid it on the ground. Using her sheath knife, she cut a section of green parachute cord and used that to tie the flare to the bottom log, only inches from the shavings. The device was triggered by a sharp tug on a ring at the end and the label said it would burn for about five minutes. She probably didn't even need the magnesium, but wanted to be sure of a start.

At first, Kit thought the wood would be too light to provide a good anchor for the flare but when she pulled smartly on the orange tube, she found the logs barely moved. Next, she tied the end of her spool of fishing line to the pull-trigger ring of the flare and trailed it across the five or so feet of rocky ground and low scrub of blueberry brush to the edge of the small bluff. Peering over to make sure the small plastic spool wouldn't hang up on anything, she let it drop.

Before following it down herself, Kit took the tattered remains of one of the space blankets out of her pocket and unfolded it across the top of the wood pile. The wind blew steadily as she worked, whipping and tearing at the silver sheet. By lifting a log here and a stick there, she was able to tuck the blanket into a sort of tarp over the top of the signal pyre. She hoped the covering would stay in place long enough to keep it dry until they needed it. A hot fire would burn away the thin Mylar immediately but Kit made sure to leave plenty of open area at the base for air to get to the blaze in case it took longer than she thought.

In the grey light of mid-morning the fishing line was all but invisible against the steep wall of rough stone and moss. Down by the creek, Kit had to look for several seconds to locate it and then only found it because of the white plastic spool lying on a clump of willows above one of her wire snares. She was gratified to see the lifeless body of a snowshoe hare hanging in the snare, its brown fur coat already blotchy white anticipating the approach of winter. She'd checked all the snares as soon as she left the mine and they were empty. This one must have been sprung while she was building the fire. Taking the plump rabbit out of the wire, she laid it on the ground and reset the trap. The fishing line hung along the hillside among the willows above the snare and once Kit removed the spool, it was well camouflaged.

Kit picked up the supper and her rifle, surveying her work. With the fishing line trigger in place either she or Paul would be able to start the fire without having to take the extra time to climb the hill. Though rabbit didn't have enough fat to be the most nutritious meat in the world, she was sure it would help Terry and raise everyone's spirits. She decided to pick a few more berries before going back to the mine; the sugar in them seemed to do good things for Terry. The constant breeze did a good job of keeping the bugs at bay and though a few still hummed around her ears, fighting the wind, she paid them no mind.

Happy at having accomplished her planned tasks, Kit strolled along the bank of the small stream looking for a likely berry crop where she could sit and pick without getting up to move. She'd only gone a few steps when she saw a succulent clump of bright green leaves growing at the water's edge. She couldn't remember the name of the plant, but felt certain it was what her mother used as a poultice to draw out infections. Smiling to herself, she set the gun and rabbit down on the ground beside the bushes. The plants grew away from the bank, almost in the middle, and Kit had to grab a handful of willow branches to keep from falling in to the gurgling water.

Hanging onto the slender branches and leaning out over the mossy bank, Kit suddenly froze. She'd left the gun, her only means of protection behind her, and though she couldn't put her finger on exactly what it was, she knew something, or someone was back there with it. Something sweaty. Something dangerous.

By late afternoon, Paul was past panic and had worked himself into a state of numb, pessimistic worry. His friend lay, clinging to life at the back of the mine, shivering like he had pneumonia; the prisoner continued to stare at him, making crude threats and telling him how Terry wouldn't make it through another night—and now Kit had not come back. More than anything, Paul wanted to go check on her, but he felt it would be wrong to leave Terry. She had been gone for more that five hours and he was getting very thirsty since she had both water bottles. He rationalized that he should go find her to get some water for Terry, but the thought of the scar nosed-Russian kept him in the mine.

Standing at the entrance, the boy wracked his brain, trying to think of something to do that wouldn't get him and Terry killed—something that wasn't stupid. He tried to think of what Kit would do and decided he should wait awhile longer.

Leon's feet were still tied in hobbles. He couldn't take the chance that the boy might catch him trying to escape and break his knees with the pick handle. But his hands were free. By working at the parachute cord one string at a time, he'd been able to use the tiny grouse bone to pop loose the bonds without arousing Paul's suspicions.

But even with free hands, the outlaw had to wait until the right time to make his move. Even though the marshal had a bad fever and lapsed in and out of consciousness, the guy still had the pistol somewhere under his blanket, and there was too much of a chance he might have time to use it. If he believed anything at all, Dahl believed Terry would keep his promise to kill him. He was sure the boy would try. Leon didn't intend to give either one of them the chance. At first, he'd been happy when Kit hadn't returned. She was just one more person to worry about when he tried to escape. But the longer she was absent, the more he worried that Vasilii had gotten her and was at that very moment beating information as to his whereabouts out of her. He'd known Vasilii and his stooge Adrik long enough to be sure that once they had someone in their grasp, they knew countless ways to get information. For a while he actually wished Kit would return. At least then he would know Petrov didn't have her.

But she didn't, and Leon worked himself into a lather, fully expecting to see Petrov step into the dark room at any moment. It was this desperate fear that finally drove him to action.

The boy couldn't seem to stand still and spent most of his time pacing back and forth with the pick handle closer to the entrance looking for the girl. Leon couldn't afford to move with the kid behind him, but luckily he came back every few minutes to check on the sick marshal, bending over to check his temperature, as if checking him might somehow make him better. The outlaw chose one of those moments to make his move.

When Paul's back was turned, Dahl gathered himself up against the support beam that had been his prison and sprang against the boy, knocking him on top of Terry. He'd hoped to get the pistol right away but his legs had turned to rubber from so many hours in the same position and he fell after his first lunge.

The weight of Paul's body impacted Terry like a sack of rocks and he cried out in pain and surprise. Pushing out with his good arm, he shoved Paul off him before realizing who he was, then struck out at what looked like Dahl's face lying by his foot. In the melee, Terry lost control of the pistol and it skittered across the rocky floor, disappearing into the darkness. Driven by desperation, Leon was up again in an instant and staggering from a kick to the chin, swung at Paul savagely with all his might. The blow caught the boy square in the side of the face and sent him sprawling back against the far wall where he sank in a motionless heap.

The outlaw had spent hours over the last three days doing nothing but watching Terry. He knew exactly where the worst injuries were and did his best to exploit them. Still not sure where the pistol was, Dahl turned on Terry quickly after he'd dealt with Paul, sending a brutal kick to the injured man's broken ribs. The blow connected, but just barely as Leon's legs were jerked out from underneath him and he remembered he was still hobbled. He recovered quickly, and rolled on top of Terry's injured side, using both fists to pummel the lawman's broken ribs.

Terry choked back the urge to vomit and used the intense pain of the beating to help clear the fog in his head. In training, he often fought on the ground. Sometimes he fought with only one arm so he wasn't totally without technique. His main problem was one of strength. Holds that should have sent Dahl flying, merely staggered him and punches that a week before would have rendered the outlaw unconscious if they didn't kill him, only served to keep him at bay.

When Dahl jumped on his injured ribs, Terry was able to roll slightly out of the way to keep his lungs from being punctured and delivered a blinding stiff-armed thumb directly into his opponent's eye. Dahl sprang back clawing at his eye and screeching in pain.

Then he saw the pick handle. That was all he needed to finish the fight. Terry slid his good hand along the floor in the darkness, frantically searching for the pistol but it wasn't there. Dahl grinned a wide, jagged grin as he hefted the thick piece of hickory and tested it against his open palm with a resounding slap. "Pitiful," he said and raised the heavy club over his head to deliver a skull-crushing blow … but his words turned into shrieking howl.

The wood fell limply to the ground and Dahl staggered as half his left ear was ripped from the side of his head. The second shot struck at the base of his neck below the skull, and sent the man to his knees. Screaming in agony, Dahl clawed at the searing pain in the back of his neck. Blood gushed between his fingers as he clutched what was left of his ear. When he was first hit, Leon was sure Vasilii had shot him. He'd never been shot, but assumed it would hurt as much as he hurt at that very moment. But what he saw scared him almost as bad as Petrov.

Paul quickly reloaded and stood framed and backlit by the mine entrance, his vine maple slingshot up and ready for another shot. He was breathing slowly, taking his time now that his target was down. A thin trickle of blood oozed from the corner of his mouth where Leon had hit him. His eyes locked in narrow slits, burning a hole in Dahl. He'd rushed the first two shots to keep the man from killing Terry with the pick handle. Now, he could relax a degree and take more careful aim. He had enough faith in his ability with the weapon to know he could put Dahl down for good with one well-placed stone to the head. Especially at this range. "Just like David and Goliath," he said under his breath.

Leon's bloody hand shot up to cover his head and he ducked low to avoid the next zinging rock that he knew would certainly kill him.

"Paul." Terry's voice was calm but ragged. He had found the gun in the darkness and had it trained on the cowering outlaw. "It's all right, I have him now."

"No," Paul screamed. "He was going to kill you." Then the boy's voice grew quiet, the way his father's had when he was angry. His hands stayed steady, ready to finish Dahl. "Just like they killed my father. No one ever came out and told me but I can read the papers. I know men just like this one beat my father to death with a piece of pipe." He took a slow, deep breath, deepening his resolve. "People like these don't deserve to live. He would have killed you and then me. And then what would have happened to my mother?"

Dahl cowered lower against the ground, whimpering. "Come on Paul, please…" It was the first time, he'd used the boy's real name. "I'm sorry." His voice was strained and choked with sobs.

"I'm not going to lie to you," Terry said, using his knee to keep the pistol leveled at Dahl. "If I gave this gun to him right now he'd still kill us both. He may not deserve to live, but you don't deserve to live with having killed him. If he needs to be killed, I'll do it." Terry sighed. "Your father was a great man, Paul. Be like him, not this garbage."

CHAPTER 24

Adrik had often used the smoke of partisan fires to track his enemy in Afghanistan. Humans had an aversion to raw meat and though they might forgo a warming fire, they invariably built at least a small one to cook with. The narrow trickle hadn't been much, and hadn't lasted long but it was more than enough to turn the big Russian in the right direction. Once he had a general location, it had only been a matter of time.

Kit let herself get too far away from the rifle and now she was going to pay. Before she could turn around, she heard Vasilii Petrov's wolf whistle as he walked up behind her with a cruel smirk on his face.

"Stupid girl!" he spat and kicked her headlong into the stream.

Kit floundered in the frigid water, slipping twice on the greasy, moss-covered rocks as she got back to her feet. She didn't intend to fight, but she wasn't going to stay in the water any longer than she had to. Raising her hands above her dripping head in surrender, she stepped back onto the bank. "I suppose I've been expecting …"

"Shut up," Vasilii screamed, spit flying from his twisted mouth. The jagged white scar across his nose stood out in sharp contrast to the red flush of anger throbbing across his face. "Where is Leon? Tell me at once." Before she could answer, he slapped her across the cheek with the back of his hand.

"He's dead." Kit rubbed her swelling jaw and glared at the fuming Russian, dark, angry tears welling up in her eyes.

"Dead?" Petrov's chin dropped. "How could he be dead?"

"He tried to escape and killed the boy and man I was with, so I killed him. I'm all alone now."

Vasilii grabbed a handful of hair on both sides of his head and rocked back and forth in exasperation. Adrik who had merely smiled so far during the confrontation stepped forward.

"How very convenient for you, my dear. For your sake, I hope Mr. Dahl is still alive and able to answer our questions." The big Russian's English was flawless. Had it not been for the cruel sneer crossing his bug-bitten, wind-chapped face, he would have seemed courteous. His polite, condescending attitude frightened and angered Kit at the same time.

"I don't know what to tell you." Kit knew she was as good as dead anyway, so drastic action was warranted. Her mind raced wildly trying to think of some way out. At the very least she had to warn Paul. A scream might do it but a boy like him would come to investigate.

Adrik shrugged and rubbed his large hands together in front of him. "I knew you would take some convincing, *doporoi*." My darling. "I have waited patiently for the time I would be able to do the convincing myself."

"Enough of this talk," Vasilii screamed, stepping in close to Kit so his crooked nose was only an inch from her face. "You will tell me what I want to know or I will shoot you on this spot."

Kit had no choice but to keep up the lie and buy time. "I buried them all about two miles down the mountain. Covered them really, because of the permafro …"

"Liar!" Petrov swung out savagely, harder than before sending Kit sprawling over a clump of willows, blood pouring from her nose. Before she could get up he was standing over her, kicking her mercilessly in the ribs. Turning on her side, she rolled into a ball trying to protect her face and sides as best she could. Then, through the flurry of kicks she saw the fishing line hidden among the willow shrubs, dangling down the face of the hill from the signal fire above. She reached to pull it but the point of Petrov's shoe caught her in the shoulder and sent a paralyzing jolt of pain down the side of her body. Falling over on her back, she clawed at the bushes at her side as if trying to get to her feet.

To Kit, the world seemed to be moving in slow motion. She was aware of Petrov kicking her; of his high-pitched, almost feminine screaming, of the darker, big Russian smiling and rubbing his bushy mustache as if he was amused by her beating. The fishing line she used for her trigger was heavy stuff and she was afraid if she yanked too hard it might pull the whole pile of wood down on top of her—but it really didn't matter, a few more kicks and she would be unconscious anyway, or dead. She jerked the line with all her strength, but nothing happened. From her vantage point on the ground she couldn't actually see the signal fire but pulling the line was like pulling against a two-ton rock. Then she began to fear she might break the line, that it might have become tangled around a shrub or rock and wasn't pulling on the flare at all. But she pulled anyway. Two more stout yanks, and the line fell free.

Petrov stopped kicking her. One of his shoes had flown off in his effort and he was leaning forward, hands on his knees to catch his breath. His big toe stuck from a hole in the grimy white sock. Adrik still stood back, looking down at her with his head cocked to one side, studying her reaction to the beating. At first Kit thought she'd been right and the line had broken, but staring up at Petrov's twisted sweating face she saw bits of the melted space blanket swirling thirty feet above him. Pieces of black ash carried by the wind high above to the gathering clouds. It had worked. The fire started on the first pull and when it was going well, burned the line away allowing it to pull free. Neither Russian noticed the grey-white smoke billowing up above their heads.

Kit turned her head to the side panting in relief. It would not do her any good, but if anyone was near, they might see the smoke and be able to save Paul from these animals. Animals. That's exactly what they were—exactly what Dahl was, for getting them into this mess to begin with. Animals that needed to be hunted down and dealt with before they could do any more harm. The beat of her heart throbbed painfully in the back of her head and Kit was only vaguely aware that Petrov was speaking to her again. Questioning—no, demanding to know where Dahl was hiding. Coughing, she tried to clear her head. They were going to kill her, she knew that. She just didn't know how. The one with the scarred nose might kill her accidentally but she was pretty sure from the bigger one's eyes he didn't want it to happen that way.

"All right you stupid, pitiful thing," Vasilii panted, his hands still on his knees. "You will tell us what I want to know this minute or I will let my friend Adrik have a go with you. I assure you he knows how to bring a tear from a turnip and I will have my information." His voice rose again in agitation and froth flew from his mouth. "Where is Dahl?"

Kit was on her side, curling to prepare for another flurry of kicks when her eye caught the snare. The thin, sharp wire that would cut through unprotected skin like butter, hung in the branches, only inches from Vasilii's shoe-less right foot. If he kicked at her now he might miss the loop.

"Okay, you win." Kit raised a hand in surrender, wincing at the pain. Moving slightly to her left, she rose to her feet. "I'll tell you where he is ..." Her eyes narrowed and she spat in the Russian's face. "After I see you rot on this mountain." Kit dropped into a ball on the ground waiting for the kick she knew would come, but it never hit her.

The jolt of the thin wire catching his bare ankle sent Petrov over backward and he fell with a thud onto the rocky ground. He couldn't figure out what had him, and though he didn't have any experience with such things, thought he might have been bitten by a snake. Still not realizing he was caught, the shrieking Russian tried to sit up but that just pulled the snare deeper into the tender pale skin above his sock. Each time the wire cut he thrashed. Each time he kicked the wire cut.

Kit heard Adrik laugh out loud as she sprang to her feet and first limped, then ran for the small pocket of birches across the mountain stream. She was already soaking wet so the water didn't bother her and amazingly she kept her feet across the greasy, moss-covered rocks. Adrik still had the rifle and as long as she remained in the open he could shoot her. Kit's shoulders and hips had taken the brunt of Petrov's beating and they screamed at her as she ran. If she could only make it to the trees she might be able to get away or at least lure the big man further away from the others.

Behind her, she heard Petrov cry out in hysterical agony for his comrade Adrik. Chancing a quick glance over her shoulder, she saw the big Russian, rifle in hand coming after her at a steady trot. He was not more than fifty yards away when she made the trees. Kit ran without looking back, dodging back and forth to avoid thick underbrush, almost hypnotized by the white trunks swaying in the gathering wind like seaweed in an ocean. Looking around her as she ran and stumbled through the forest she searched for a way to distance herself from her pursuer—to escape.

Her lungs burned; her legs wobbled underneath her. The point of her left hip was beginning to stiffen and she slowed in spite of herself. Then he hit her. The blow was soft—as if he didn't want to damage her further—only stop her from running. Kit hit the ground rolling across her injured shoulder then collapsing in a heap at the base of a birch sapling.

Kit clenched her eyes shut, fully expecting a bullet at any moment to end her suffering and pain. When none came, she opened one eye and remembered what Vasilii Petrov had said about his companion. He could get a tear from a turnip. Of course he wouldn't shoot her, he still wanted to know where Dahl had the money. Instead of pointing the rifle at her, Adrik had leaned it against a nearby tree and drawn a long thick-bladed knife from his belt.

Tapping the side of the glinting blade on his open palm, the powerful Russian smiled. "I can see you are a strong one; a worthy opponent for me. But it has been my experience that women begin to talk by the time I remove the second finger." The twisted smile faded from his lips and he took a slow deliberate step. Kit tried to get up and run—then crawl, but it was no use. He would catch her anyway, there was absolutely nothing she could do. She had been in dozens of frightening, even life-threatening situations before; but looking up at the heartless man with his wild mustache and inhuman eyes, Kit was immobilized by fear.

CHAPTER 25

Skip wished they were tracking horses. At least they left definite footprints. Terry had sworn up and down that anyone who walked anywhere left some kind of sign behind, but Skip was beginning to have serious doubts. They'd been working along the moraine for over an hour, hoping they were on the right trail. There were tracks, or at least divots in the gravel that looked like tracks all along the natural highway. Skip and Mac agreed that more than likely they'd been made by Terry and the others but they were really no more than shapeless gouges in the gravel so it was impossible to be sure. Until they got to the river.

Tracks lined the muddy bank and it was easy to see where Terry had rested next to a large rock, his Danner boot prints clearly visible in the dirt. Mac sighed with relief when he found Kit's smaller boot prints and pointed out Paul's prints that moved back and forth several times between Terry's and Kit's.

"This set doesn't have a very long stride for someone with feet this big," Skip got off his horse to study a larger set of boot prints and thought how much he sounded like Terry. In between some of the impressions, particularly where they crossed soft mud there was a telltale scuffing as if the trackee was dragging something. Skip tipped back his hat and rubbed his beard, thinking. "I'll bet this is our outlaw and Terry has him hobbled," he said, slapping his knee and startling the paint horse in the process. "Sorry Havoc, don't be gettin' mad at me now."

Belle scampered back and forth checking out the various tracks with her nose. Her ears perked and she whined when she found the place where Terry had sat. She circled the area three times, then lay down on the cool ground as if to think. The mosquitoes were worse along the river where the wind wasn't as strong and the little blue dog had to keep snuffling to keep them off her nose.

"This isn't good news," Roberson said under his breath, barely loud enough for Skip to hear. "It's not necessarily bad news but no, it's definitely not good."

"What?" Skip stood up expecting to see a dead body from Roberson's tone of voice. "What's not good news?"

"Come see for yourself." The Mountie was standing over a mud flat the river had washed over the gravel bar. Belle's ears perked up from the urgency in his voice and she padded softly toward where he stood. Ten feet away a swirling breeze brought the scent of what he was looking at and the dog began to growl, hackles raised like a young lion.

"Holy smokes," Skip whistled when he came up beside his dog. "I hope that's not what I think it is."

"If you think it's a grizzly bear then I'm afraid you're dead on." Roberson was busy measuring the track with his hands. "And a big one at that, almost three hands wide. But I'm not so much worried about his size."

"Me either," Skip nodded fingering the safety on his shotgun to make himself feel better. "I'm worried he might have a taste for paint horses."

"Look at this. I'm no tracker but I'd say this grizzly put his foot down on top of this print of Kit's wouldn't you?"

Skip handed Havoc's reins to the Mountie but kept the shotgun and knelt beside him. "Sure enough, Mr. Bear stepped smack dab on top of her track and squished it down." Skip was amazed at how the small human footprint seemed so puny and insignificant compared to the huge clawed track of the grizzly.

Leading the horses, Mac took a few steps down the bank. "Now this is bad news."

"More bear sign?"

"Exactly. More tracks just like that one." Skip followed Belle who was already sniffing at a line that headed up the nearest hill. The whole group had used this route to the mountains—and so had the bear.

"At least we know the way they went," Skip said, smiling weakly.

Once they left the river bottom and the moraine the trail disappeared completely. Even Belle was not sure which way to go on the folding, up-and-down terrain. Each new crest brought a dozen possible new directions to follow. The wind kicked up strong enough to bend the brim of Skip's felt hat and he had to fix the stampede string snugly behind his head to keep it from blowing off and sailing like a silver-belly frisbee down the lonely mountainside.

Roberson proved to be just as eager as Skip and just as lacking in the tracking department.

"I thought you Mounties were supposed to be experts in wilderness wisdom, always getting your man and all." Skip kept a close eye on the paint horse as he talked. So far it hadn't bucked, but there was a lot of riding left to do and as a rule horses didn't seem to like riding in the wind.

Mac looked up from the ground and reined in his horse. "I could say the same about you marshals."

"I haven't seen a shred of sign in quite some time. We could be riding right by the ridge they're camped behind." Skip sank into his saddle. They were riding up a long, narrow gap in the hills, watching Belle when she took a particular trail but going mainly by instinct. Seeing Belle stop to snoop at a side trail, Skip suddenly climbed down from his horse. "Are you a prayin' man Constable Roberson?" He'd been brooding for miles about Rockwell's visit and all the advice the old gunfighter had given him. Exasperated about not finding a solid trail he finally decided he didn't care if the Mountie laughed in his face, he had to do something besides wander around the Yukon hoping to run into his friends or the bear that ate them.

Mac shrugged. "I'm not adverse to a talk with the Almighty, if that's what you mean. To be quite honest with you, I've been having a little chat within myself for the past few days. It is my girlfriend out there, eh."

"Well, get down here then and let's get to it. I'm worried and I need a direction to go in."

The prayer helped—as it always did, but as usual there were no bolts of lightning or flaming arrows pointing the way. At the very least Skip hoped Port might come and whisper in his ear but so far the guardian angel hadn't offered so much as a peep.

Then Belle growled. A low, deep rumble that sent a shiver down Skip's spine. Belle wasn't the kind of dog who got scared of much. When Skip first moved to Montana, she'd even attacked his chain saw while he was bringing in the first winter's wood. Skip didn't want to meet up with anything that scared a dog who would attack a chain saw.

A split second after Belle growled, Havoc decided it was time to commence his bucking routine for the day. The horse's first jump slammed Skip's thighs into the swells of his saddle and his belly against the horn. He jammed his feet forward in the stirrups and narrowly escaped going off the front. Before he could get a good seat, the long-necked horse spun and reared, the bony spot between its ears catching Skip squarely in the forehead. Bogging its head, the paint continued across the side hill in a series of bone-rattling, jaw-clomping lunges.

Skip was never one to get heavy-handed with his riding, but out of the corner of his eye, he could see just a few feet up the trail what had scared the animals, and this bucking had to stop. Gathering as much leather as he could between jumps, Skip yanked for all he was worth with his right hand and jerked the big paint's nose around so it touched his knee. Now the horse had two choices; quit bucking or buck blindly until it fell down. Bull Witherspoon might ride a horse with a quirk or two but he wouldn't keep one that wasn't smart. Once it was clear that Skip had his head, Havoc quit pitching and stood quivering on the hillside. Belle, who'd been worried about her man on the horse, stood at his feet now growling and waiting for the order that would release her into action.

Mac was barely controlling Raven and goaded the horse harshly with his heels to keep him from completely swapping ends and heading for home. "I was afraid you were going to come off," the Mountie whispered, keeping his horse facing the trail. "You'd think these horses had never seen a bear before."

Once he got his horse to stop jigging he was able to see what Mac was talking about. Not thirty yards away stood the biggest grizzly he had ever imagined. The bear stood on his hind legs and moved his keg-sized head back and forth like a curious dog trying to figure out the men and horses. Skip judged him to be ten feet tall since it seemed that sitting on the horse the man and bear were looking just about eye to eye. Without warning the huge grizzly dropped to all fours and swatted at the ground with a forepaw the size of a shovel, throwing up a cloud of dust.

Skip thumbed off the shotgun's safety with a loud click, suddenly glad he had more than a pistol. Roberson heard the click and slowly held up his open hand. "Be careful and see what he's going to do first. If you shoot him you might make him really mad, eh."

"What he's going to do is eat the one of us that's slowest gettin' out of here." Skip softly patted Havoc on the front shoulder, trying to calm him. Both horses had seen the bear and stood hypnotized, muscles twitching, coiled and ready to explode. Skip knew enough about bears to know that he couldn't outrun one on a reliable horse—which Havoc was not. The big grizzly could cover the thirty yards between them in a matter of seconds; one or two good bounds really. He knew all that in his mind, but it was still awfully difficult to think about anything but running.

"If he charges, I'm going to shoot." Skip whispered, winding a hand around his reins.

"That should make it easier for him to get acquainted when that horse throws you on these rocks. He might just be bluffing us."

Skip nodded. He'd faced crazed killers and many different types of cold-blooded outlaw monsters but he'd never faced anything ten feet tall with claws as long as his fingers, so he yielded to the expert. "Bluffing. Bluffing would be good. I think I should tell him I'm older than you and therefore have much more gristle."

The bear rose up again and sniffed the air, then seemed to relax and flopped down on the ground like a dog with his chin on his front paws. He almost looked like he was going to sleep.

"You think he's daring us to move?" Skip said, glancing at the

Mountie out of the corner of his eye.

"He doesn't want us to come that way, that's for sure. Let's see what he does if we try to go around him."

Now Skip put up his hand. "Hold on. You mean way around him right? Not just tiptoe around him on the trail."

"I'm as scared as you are. I mean around this whole hill."

The horses were glad to move out and be going away from the bear. Both men wanted to keep their horses facing the animal and backed and sidestepped down the hill. It wasn't until they had put two hundred yards between them and the still resting bear that Mac turned his horse and let him step out on his own. They were at the base of a hogback ridge and once they went around it the bear was out of sight and a whole new valley opened up in front of them. Both men stopped at the same instant when they rounded the jutting face of rock. What they saw immediately caused them to forget the bear. A quarter mile away, up a long narrow draw a thick plume of smoke curled skyward from the top of a mesa-like shelf.

Thankful for the bear sending them in the right direction, each man prayed again, but this time they didn't kneel. They had friends that needed help and now they were close. The Lord would understand if they gave thanks at the gallop

CHAPTER 26

The ground around Vasilii Petrov was stained dark red. The thin wire had sliced through the tender flesh above his sock and buried itself next to the bone. He knew he was likely to lose his foot, if he didn't die, and cursed Adrik for running away and leaving him just to go after the girl, but consoled himself with the sure knowledge that his friend would make the insolent woman pay for what she had done to him.

At first his anger at Kit and hate of Dahl were all that kept him conscious but the pain grew so intense it gradually ate away at all his other emotions until it filled him completely and left room for nothing but self-pity. When he looked up at the bluff above him and saw the smoke from Kit's signal fire, the fear of getting caught cut through him as quickly as the snare wire. After a short time, when it began to dawn on him that he would die without help, he began to worry that no one would see the smoke. When he weighed the options of a lonely, painful death on a Canadian mountainside or going to prison with one foot, there didn't seem to be much of a choice.

Petrov pulled his sock back and looked at the thin, scalpel-like cut above his ankle. There wouldn't be much work for the surgeon that had to cut it off, he chuckled morbidly to himself, half giddy from the loss of so much blood. Then he began to laugh out loud, quietly at first—only a whisper of a laugh, then the demented hysterical giggle of a man who had resigned himself to death.

He was laughing maniacally, picking at the embedded wire when Skip and Mac rode up behind him. Belle looked up at Skip for direction and whined at the copper smell of blood and fear. Skip whispered to reassure her and she lay down on the edge of the cool stream bank understanding that the wounded man before her was the enemy but no longer a threat.

Roberson saw the man's face first and whistled under his breath at all the blood. "Petrov, I presume," he said looking at Skip and nodding at the scar on the Russian's nose. The Mountie dismounted and looped Raven's reins around a willow branch. "Looks like you're in some pain, eh," Roberson said as he took the pistol from Petrov's waistband, cleared it and stuck it in his own belt. The Russian looked at him with wild, other-worldly eyes and laughed. He spoke in slurred Russian, picking at the wire around his foot.

"Don't," Roberson scolded, tapping on his arm. "You'll bleed to death if you bother with that too much."

"Let's not let him bleed to death before we find out if that's more than his blood on the ground here," Skip said turning Havoc on his haunches to get a three-hundred-and- sixty degree view of his surroundings. "You speak English?" Skip's voice was rough and full of contempt.

"Da," Petrov giggled. "Do not worry; my friend, Adrik will take care of them for us. I do not know if he will come back for me but he will take care of that traitor Dahl."

"Which way did Adrik go?" Skip tried to play along with the wounded man's delirium but the Russian's eyes narrowed into a skeptical glare and he stopped laughing.

"I think I shall surely lose my foot," he said.

"Which way did Adrik go?" Skip could see tracks all over the bank of the small stream. He could tell there had been a serious scuffle but he couldn't find anything to give him a direction of travel. Petrov knew, he just couldn't seem to hold a thought between his ears long enough to get it into words.

"Think, man," Roberson patted the Russian on the cheeks. He was a little rough about it which impressed Skip a great deal. "Tell us which way."

Vasilii nodded groggily as if he finally understood what the men were asking, but before he could open his mouth his eyes rolled back in their sockets and he collapsed against into

Roberson's arms. The Mountie reached around and pressed two fingers against the man's neck.

"His pulse is weak, but it's still there," he pronounced and stood up to retrieve a first aid kit with bandages from Raven's saddle bag. "I'm going to have to do something about his leg or he'll die." There was an air of anxiousness in the Mountie's voice. Duty wouldn't let him allow the prisoner to die, but his girlfriend was still out there somewhere in great danger.

"If I could figure out which way to go, I'd go take care of this Adrik character once and for all," Skip said, reading Roberson's mood. Belle was up around again, sniffing at this track and that track and Skip studied her movements to see if she might provide him a clue. If the dog caught a scent she recognized she gave no indication so Skip turned his attention back to the ground. "Do you see anything?"

Roberson was busy trying to fashion a tourniquet from a long piece of bandage and a stick. There wasn't one in the first-aid kit. In fact, there was a small laminated card with a warning against using such a thing but whoever had made the card hadn't faced the realities of practicing medicine in the wilderness. The bleeding started up again in earnest and there was no choice in the matter. Petrov could either bleed to death or lose the leg. Roberson realized that in the old days of the RCMP, he would have been expected to take off the leg himself, for there would have been no one else. He looked up at Skip from his bloody work. "I'll help you look as soon as I get this done. Can't see anything from here."

Skip lifted Havoc's reins and stopped the horse in mid-stride. Of course. In his haste to catch the outlaws and save the day, he'd wasted time by not getting out of the saddle. He remembered his father telling him once that he spent so much time horseback it was starting to make his brain sore.

When he slid to the ground, he gave the horse his head and let him get a well-deserved drink from the little mountain stream—and there it was. On such a cloudy day with the wind and current whipping up the surface of the water it was impossible to see the tracks from the higher angle of the saddle. Just beneath the surface the light green traces of footprints shimmered and danced across the moss covered rocks where someone had crossed. As sure as a compass needle they pointed in a straight line across the water and Skip followed them, dragging the horse through the water after him. Once he was sure the tracks went all the way to the other side, he looked up and saw the shimmering stand of birch trees. He still had the shotgun but needed only one arm to swing back into the saddle.

"I think they're headed for the trees," he shouted. "I'm going ahead. Radio for help then meet me over there when you're done." He figured Roberson would give him a lecture on a U.S. Marshal's lack of authority in Canada. Instead the Mountie stood and took the revolver from his belt. He held it butt first toward the deputy.

"You might need this, eh."

Skip snorted a laugh and shook his head. "No time to trade," he said over his shoulder, itching to get on the trail now that he had it in his sights. "Besides," he held the shotgun out to his side. "I believe my hand's grown permanently attached to this thing." Skip ordered Belle to stay with the Mountie as he turned. Quivering like a tightly wound clock she grudgingly obeyed.

Roberson watched Skip spur the big paint horse into a lope across the mountainside and redoubled his efforts to get the tourniquet set and Petrov handcuffed so he could join the fight.

Once the tracks left the streambed they disappeared completely but Skip didn't let that slow him down. He had a line of travel and when he neared the underbrush and scrub that ran along the tree line he could easily see where the branches parted and something big, something human-sized, ran through.

Golden brown birch leaves fell from the trees like rain when Skip urged Havoc into the grey white forest. He quickly realized he was going to have to dismount to get anywhere unnoticed. The leaves and ground litter would trumpet the horse's movements like a bugler sounding the charge. So far he had the wind in his face. That helped some with the sound, but he didn't want to take any chances. Tying the horse to a tree, Skip took a few steps forward and scanned the woods in front of him. He thought he heard voices on the wind and strained to pick out where they came from.

With all the debris on the ground it was actually much easier to track in the forest and Skip inched forward, following the scuff marks in the loose debris and dirt. He stopped every few steps and sniffed the air, listening for the voices and scanning the shadows. The Russian was off to one side when Skip first caught a glimpse of him and immediately the deputy went deeper into his hunting mode—move a step, stop and assess the situation, move a step, then stop again.

When he was thirty yards away, Skip got a good look at what was going on and realized the gravity of the situation. Adrik had bound Kit's feet and stood her next to a sturdy birch. One hand was tied to the belt at her waist and he held the other, palm out, at face level against the tree, while he ran the tip of his knife along the edge of the trembling girl's chin. The wind, sifting through the quaking birch leaves helped hide Skip's approach, but it was easy to see the big Russian was so preoccupied with the power he exerted over the poor woman that he was oblivious to everything else around him. As far as he knew, he was in complete control.

Skip thought sure he could sneak up behind the bully and bust him on the head with the butt of the shotgun but didn't want to take a chance on the girl getting cut. Blood already mixed with her tears where Adrik had given her a small superficial cut on the cheek.

The Russian placed the blade over the knuckle of Kit's little finger and smiled softly, cocking his head a little to one side. His voice was almost kind as if he were pointing out some landmark in his country to a visiting friend. "I am going to ask you a few questions and then I will remove your baby finger. It is important that you understand, even if you tell me what I want to know, your own behavior has cost you at least one finger."

Kit sucked in her breath and her shoulders began to shake uncontrollably.

"United States Marshals! Throw down the knife," Skip shouted to get the Russian's attention away from Kit. He'd hoped she would fall to the ground and out of the way but Adrik grabbed her around the chest and pulled her in front of him, holding the tip of the razor-sharp blade against her bare throat. The outlaw's eyes shot to the rifle a few feet away leaning against a tree. It was too far—for the moment. Smiling, the man shook his head at Skip. "If you shoot with that cannon you will kill us both, Mr. Cowboy. I do not think that is what you really want, yes?" The Russian's voice was thick with adrenaline and contempt.

Skip winked at the girl, trying to calm her and show he had the situation in hand. His deep Texas drawl sounded surprisingly calm, even to him. "I sure am glad you speak English. I thought

I might to have to kill you to make my point." If the other man had had a gun instead of a knife, Skip's options would have been much more limited. As it was, he had a little room to maneuver. "I'm close Mister, real close, and close is unlucky for you. All thirteen pellets stay pretty tight at this range." Skip had the gaping maw of the shotgun pointed directly at the pair and Kit's eyes bugged when she realized Skip was contemplating sharpshooting with the scatter gun.

"You could never be certain," Adrik scoffed at the idea. "You would just as easily hit the girl. You must let me walk out of here. That is your only choice."

"Can't do that." Skip smiled. "Tell you what I will do, though. I'm not much in a killin' mood today so I'll prove it to you." Skip kept the shotgun pointed directly at Adrik's head while he spoke. "You just take a look about six inches to your left."

The Russian's eyes darted but his head remained motionless.

"You see that dry little spruce cone hanging out there all by its lonesome? Now you be real still ... "

Kit clenched her eyes shut and turned her head as far right as she could. Adrik stomped his foot. "I see it. But what is the point of all this. I assure, you, if you do not ..."

A tremendous boom cut the air, filling the little grove as the spruce cone next to Adrik's head evaporated into a brown cloud. Without giving the Russian time to react, Skip racked another shell into the chamber and trained the shotgun back on his head, giving him a toothy grin. "I hate to say I told you so Mister, but I got four more shells in here and I'm about to start carvin' off little pieces of you that are stickin' out from behind the girl." Skip winked again and this time Kit winked back. "And I can pretty much guarantee it's gonna hurt a lot more than cutting off a finger."

Adrik dropped the knife, and raised his hands. "At last I have found a worthy opponent," the big Russian chuckled. "I only wish we could have met under different circumstances."

"Yeah, where you win. I think I'll pass on that count. Now, get down on the ground." Skip motioned with the gun barrel and turned his attention to Kit, who had already picked up the knife and was cutting her legs free. "You must be Kit, the famous bush pilot. I've been spending some time with a Mountie who thinks pretty highly of you."

Kit relaxed with a long sobbing sigh when she realized Mac

was somewhere nearby. "And you must be Skip, the famous deputy marshal and friend. I've been spending some time with two friends of yours." She looked at the ground and shook her head. "I'm afraid Terry's not doing so well."

"Is he shot?" Skip took a pair of handcuffs out of his back pocket and gave them to Kit. "Did this guy get ahold of him?" He glared hard at the Russian.

"No, he's not shot but he was banged up in the crash. I think his ribs are broken and he's got a pretty bad infection."

Skip nodded thoughtfully, the tip of the shotgun barrel moving up and down with his head. "Just so he's not shot. No bug can live in Terry very long and get away with it. He'll get better."

After Kit handcuffed the prisoner, Skip ordered him to his feet and relaxed a bit with the 12-gauge. "If you would be so kind as to grab that rifle there and lead the way to my friends, I would be much obliged to you."

A Canadian Armed Forces helicopter had already set down on a small wash and men in green jumpsuits were loading Petrov on a gurney when Skip and Kit returned with their Russian. Kit tried to run when she saw Roberson but her ribs and hip still pained her from Petrov's beating so the best she could do was an excited, limping shuffle.

If Mac cared that her hair looked like a ratted mess of tangled black moss, he didn't show it. Her face was filthy and swollen from hundreds of scabby insect bites so he had a difficult time finding a place to kiss her—but he did.

Kit refused to sit down until she led Skip and Mac to the mine. Her hand shot to her mouth when she saw Dahl was gone from his support post and the cavern empty. "I can't understand it, they were right ..." Then she began to chuckle when Mac played his flashlight along the back wall. Scratched into the grey stone in foot-high letters was CTR. "Choose the right," she whispered under her breath looking at the side tunnels of the main room. "I know where they went," she said, but the clue didn't matter. Belle had been doing a bit of her own investigation and gave an excited yap when she caught Terry's scent down the tunnel to the far right of the mine.

Roberson assisted other arriving RCMP with the prisoners while Skip and Paul helped get a heavily medicated Terry aboard a second helicopter. After making sure Kit was settled, the Mountie chatted briefly with two of the pilots who stood at the tail of one of the birds poring over a aeronautical chart. Clouds were beginning to unload their first few drops of rain and the men seemed in a hurry to get back in the air. At length he nodded his head and strode solemnly over to Skip, extending his hand.

"It turned out to be a real pleasure," Skip said, pumping the hand vigorously.

"Likewise. I thought you might like to know I had two other constables take the horses back to Mr. Witherspoon." Roberson folded his arms as if he had hard news. "You know deputy Garret, that I can be a bit fanatic about getting matters done by the book."

Skip raised his hand. "Doesn't matter. I've got my friends back and that's all that counts. I'm not even upset with you for getting rid of my only other means out of here besides flying."

"Well, there is something else I should tell you. I've spoken with the pilots, eh. They inform me that their navigational systems tell them that while Mr. Dahl was arrested on Canadian soil the two Russians came into custody in the United States—making them your prisoners." The Mountie gave a slight, almost formal bow. "Of course we will be glad to hold them for you in light of the unusual circumstances of their arrest until you can arrange transport to Anchorage. I'm sure there will be a few hearings."

"Why, thank you Mountie Roberson." Skip slapped the man gently on the back. "I do believe I'll take you up on that."

Kit rode out with Mac and the prisoners so Skip, Terry, and Paul had the back of the second helicopter all to themselves. The aircraft was surprisingly smooth and Skip found his nausea barely even bothered him. The copilot, who also served as a medic, had given Paul something for his shock and mild dehydration and the boy was asleep almost before they left the ground.

Skip sat with his back against the wall in a long side-seat across from Terry's gurney, Belle's head resting in his lap, and looked over at the Paul. There was something different about him. Something Skip couldn't quite put his finger on. Maybe it was the dirt, or the bug bites, or the sedation, but he somehow looked older and a little wiser than he had a week before.

Belle gave a long, wide-mouthed yawn and looked up from her resting place at Port, who sat on the other side of Skip directly behind the pilots. Both crewmen were wearing green radio headsets and didn't hear Skip when he said hello.

"Well, my work here is done." The old man said, watching the boy sleep peacefully.

Skip chuckled. "And what work was that?"

"You mean you didn't recognize me in that grizzly suit? I'm hurt." Rockwell hung his head, then looked up from the corner of his eye, grinning. "Just foolin' with you. I didn't have too much to do with the bear … or at least that's the way it will look in my official report. They tell me I'm merely an advisor and I'm not to get directly involved."

"Well, thank you."

"No sir. Thank you. I'm sorry I can't stay to tell Brother McGreggor good-bye. Would you mind giving him my regards?"

"Not at all," Skip said. "And Port … I couldn't think of a better advisor than you, eh."

Then Rockwell smiled and was gone. Skip was used to the old gunfighter's quick departures and knew he and Terry would ride with the man again. He pulled out his comb and worked it through his thick, brown mustache. Slowly, as he sat listening to the beating throb of the helicopter, it dawned on him that he had just said, *eh*. He yawned and wondered if he would develop a taste for Macintosh toffee as well.

EPILOGUE

It was only a matter of weeks before hearings were completed and Canadian authorities turned over both Russians. With a little bit of legal finagling, the U.S. Government was able to convince them to turn over Leon Dahl as well. The outlaw was a little apprehensive about being turned over to the U.S. Marshals after his experience with Deputy McGreggor but much to his relief, there wasn't a single deputy in Anchorage half as mean-looking as Terry.

The prison doctors explained to a very angry Vasilii Petrov that he wouldn't be kicking any more women. Masha Balakirev came to visit Leon and begged his forgiveness through a cascade of repentant tears. Of course he forgave her at once. He was facing many years in prison and had no one else but Masha after all. Once he looked into her green eyes, forgiving was easy.

Upon his arrival at Cook Inlet jail in Anchorage, Adrik Ivanovich was assigned to a cell with a particularly smelly giant by the name of Mordekai Yeager—who decided that he didn't care for Russians at all.

Terry's wounds healed quickly so he was able to stand and help Skip bless young Beau Terence Garret. When the proud papa held his new son up for the congregation to see, there was a grin painted on his face a mile wide and even, it seemed, a little extra curl in the handle bar of his huge mustache.

That very same Sunday, Terry had the distinct privilege of

ordaining Paul Fuller to be a deacon. Skip and Bishop Morrison stood in the circle. Terry could have sworn he felt the boy's father in the room and after all the visits from Rockwell, figured it was more probable than not.

Later, while he watched Paul pass the sacrament for the first time, standing ramrod straight, Terry saw Wallace Fuller's broad shoulders. The new deacon leaned into the pew and offered the silver tray of bread glistening brightly against his new navy slacks. Zane snuggled in close to his dad, waiting for his turn at the tray and gazed up at his young hero. "He looks like a missionary, huh," the boy whispered to his dad with a grin.

Terry nodded in agreement and held his finger to his mouth. "Shhh during the Sacrament," he said, but Zane was right. Paul took the tray and turned to the row in front of them. It wasn't noticeable to anyone that didn't know what to look for, but Terry saw it. In the hip pocket of Paul's slacks was the faint Y outline of a slingshot. Terry smiled to himself and pulled his son tight against his side. Paul would be just fine.

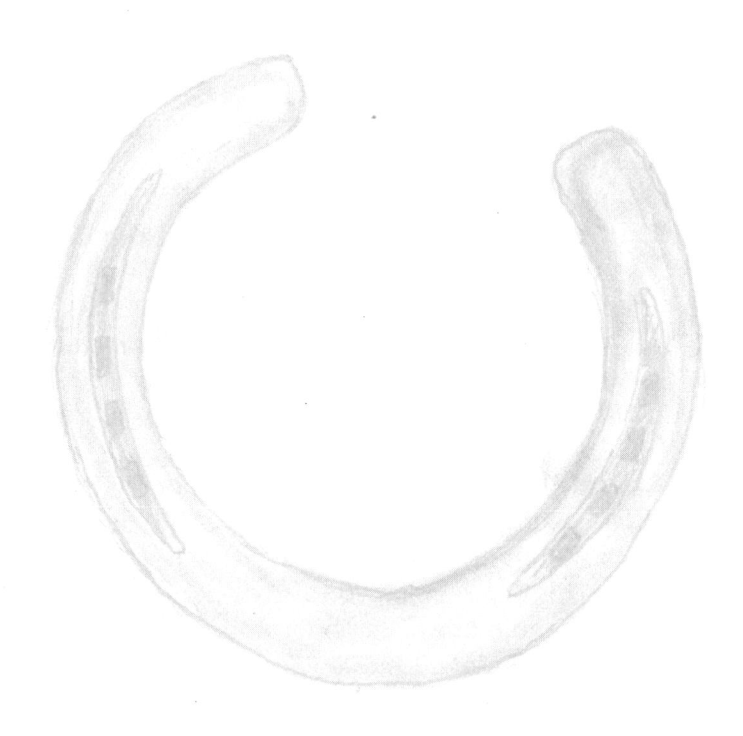